MW00915102

Curvy Nanny for the Grumpy Single Dad

A Grumpy Billionaire Sunshine Romance

Piper Sullivan

Copyright © 2024 by Piper Sullivan

All rights reserved.

No part of this book may be reproduced in any form or by any electronic or mechanical means, including information storage and retrieval systems, without written permission from the author, except for the use of brief quotations in a book review.

Enjoy Spicy Romances?

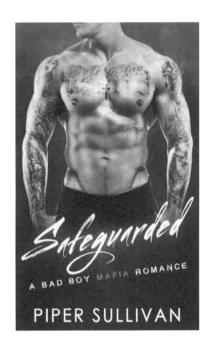

Download Safeguarded for FREE Now!

Chapter 1

Lucy

"Thanks for driving today, Luce. My head hurts like a son of a bitch." My friend and temporary roommate, Toni Stafford, gripped her head, and I could tell she was wincing even behind giant black and gold sunglasses.

I laughed and shook my head. "Drank a little too much last night?" Toni liked to have a good time when she wasn't working, and for the past week we had both been between nanny jobs.

Toni nodded, her red ponytail bounced and she froze, clutching her head once again. "It was ill-advised I know, but the Hissy Fits were playing last night, and the last two times they were in Texas I was busy working," she explained. "The only good thing about Ethan starting fifth grade is that I finally caught a live show." She'd been taking care of Ethan since he was three, but now that he was ten years old, his mom had decided that he no longer needed a nanny.

"I have painkillers in my purse. Take two and chug that bottle of water you haven't even opened yet. Serenity will flip if you show up looking hungover." Serenity Majors was our boss at the Elite Nanny Service which catered to rich parents who didn't have time for the day to day duties of parenthood. She was a good boss, but she had her limits.

Toni laughed. "I can be hungover as long as I don't look it, and that's why I made sure to look good today." She ran a hand over her ponytail. "Except the hair, I couldn't be bothered."

"You look fine," I assured her. Toni was curvy, borderline voluptuous, and she rocked it in her standard uniform of skintight jeans, plain t-shirt or tank top, and her leather jacket. She was a tough girl through and through and gave off a *don't fuck with me* vibe that I admired. "Better than fine, and you know it." Ours was an unlikely friendship, but when my last nanny job ended I had needed a place to stay, and Toni offered up her extra bedroom.

"Thanks babe, you're the best."

"I try," I assured her with a smile as traffic slowed up ahead. "Is there another event in town or something?" Our small town of Lucky was on the outskirts of Houston, so the traffic wasn't what you'd expect for a small town, but we were headed in the opposite direction of the city and traffic was still atrocious.

"Not that I know of. Probably road work, or maybe the cows or horses broke free from one of the nearby ranches."

I let out a sigh and relaxed into my seat, because one thing I learned from my time in Texas was that the animals rushed for no one. No amount of honking or wishing would get a stubborn four legged creature to move if he or she didn't want to be moved.

"All right, then. Did you meet anyone at the show last night?"

"Plenty," she grunted. "Not one of them quality material. In fact I think I need to reconsider my love of the Hissy Fits if that's the kind of men their music attracts."

I laughed and shook my head. "Or maybe *those* guys want the kind of girls the Hissy Fits' music attracts."

Toni groaned. "That makes it worse, I think."

I smiled and laughed as traffic crawled forward while Toni recounted her night of being hit on by Crypto Bros, Finance Bros and her least favorite of the bunch, *thisclose to hitting it big* wannabe musicians.

"But none of them were hot enough for a night or two?"

"That's the worst part," she scoffed. "So many of them were absolutely delicious, definitely worth a night between the sheets. But after a few minutes of one-sided conversation, I knew naked time would be just as one-sided."

"Too bad."

"What did you do last night?"

I shrugged. "I made egg rolls and fried rice, curled up on the sofa and watched...are you freaking kidding me!" A luxury red SUV crossed double lines to cut me off and then brake checked me. My abrupt stop caused the car behind me to rear end me. "Seriously!" I let out a long string of expletives that would have made my older brother and his Army buddies proud.

"Wow," Toni sighed. "That was some impressive profanity, even coming from your sweet little mouth." She laughed to herself and then stopped to clutch her head.

"This *fucking* guy," I growled and a second later I was out of my little sedan and marching towards his bright red monstrosity. I knocked on the back window, keeping my distance but fully prepared to give this jerk a piece of my mind.

The man who stepped out was the most gorgeous creature I had ever seen in my whole damn life.

Thick black hair that was slightly more stylish than his uptight suit suggested, and deep green eyes that looked like marble swirl. And the suit, designer of course, fit him perfectly to highlight his best features including his broad shoulders, long, thick thighs and a chest that was just perfect to curl up against after a long day. *Wait, what? I* blinked out of my stupor when the man took a step forward and I took a wary step back.

"What the hell is your problem?"

Long thick fingers, which I tried not to notice, raked through that thick wavy black hair and he let out a frustrated sigh. "You were going too slow." His words were deep and even, but I heard the accusation in his tone.

I had to laugh at his outrageous words. "So ten miles over the speed limit is too slow?" I felt slightly hysterical at the idea. "Another impatient businessman who thinks his time is more valuable than everybody else's. Typical." There was no use trying to make him see sense, you couldn't reason with crazy, and it was a lesson I'd had to learn the hard way over the years.

"Are you always this understanding?" He shouted the question to my back, but the amusement in his tone didn't help my mood.

"Understanding?" My feet froze and I whirled on the handsome jerk. "You want understanding because you were so impatient that you just had to get ahead by one car length, which resulted in not one, but two accidents." I pointed to the pickup truck behind me. "What I understand is that you are an entitled prick." With the sweetest smile I could muster, I arched a brow and turned away, determined to forget the good-looking jerk's face and get on with my day.

"I don't have time for this," he grumbled under his breath, and even though I knew I should've just kept going towards the waiting pickup driver, I didn't. Maybe it was the Irish on my mom's side that made me speak up, or maybe he'd just caught me on a sassy day.

I turned again with the same smile. "Just imagine, if you'd just shown a bit of patience you might be at your destination by now. Hell, all of us might be where we were headed if not for one impatient...driver. Now it's going to take *all of us* even longer to get where we were going." I smiled a little wider because taking this guy down a notch had improved my mood.

Thankfully the pickup driver was more reasonable than the hottie in the SUV, and twenty minutes later, traffic—caused by runaway cows—cleared up, and we were well on our way to Elite Nanny Service.

"Holy hell that guy was hot," Toni said eventually.

I laughed. "How long have you been waiting to let that out?"

"Since he stepped out of the car, but I wanted to give you time to calm down first."

"Thanks for that," I chuckled. "He was gorgeous. Too bad he's one of those guys who thinks the world should just move out of his way and bow to his whims."

Toni groaned. "That sucks, but to be fair, I'd totally bow before all that hotness. Naked of course."

"Of course," I repeated and rolled my eyes. "Thanks, that's just what I needed to think about for the rest of the day."

"Anytime," Toni said with a laugh as I pulled into a parking spot in the lot dedicated to Elite Nanny Service. "Now let's hope we leave this joint with new assignments."

"Serenity wouldn't have called us in otherwise, but I hope to get a long-term assignment, at least a few years." That kind of job security would be nice after a string of high paying live-in gigs. They tended to be unstable and short-lived due to job transfers and promotions that took the family away from the area, which was exactly how I found myself in search of another placement.

As we stepped inside the air conditioned building, I let my shoulders relax, and I put all thoughts of mister tall, dark and arrogant out of my mind for good.

Chapter 2

Dante

Who in the hell did that woman think she was? Yelling at me like her car getting hit was my fault. Okay so maybe it was my fault, just a little, but I needed to get home to my daughter. Lena was all alone at home, so this was an actual emergency. I didn't actually think what I had to do was more important than the next guy—or girl for that matter—but it actually *was* more important today. Anyone with children would agree with that.

I drove home at a slower pace now that I had been properly dressed down by a beautiful but annoying woman with golden hair and a sweet smile. "And that sharp tongue..." I reminded myself in the privacy of my SUV.

I couldn't help but think about the reason I was in such a hurry in the first place. The Nanny Situation, as I had started to refer to the problem I had with finding and keeping a good nanny. The nanny, well, now the ex-nanny, had upped and left in the middle of the day, with nothing but a nasty voicemail as warning. She'd abandoned my daughter all by herself in the house. Fortunately, my landscaping contractor, Billie, was on the grounds as that wretched woman had left. Billie had thankfully agreed to check in on Lena and stay on the property until I made it home to my child. Or until Dotty, our housekeeper, got back from running errands.

Why the hell was is it so hard to find a nanny who actually wanted to do her damn job? Why did every woman who showed up on my doorstep want a promotion into my bedroom? It really was unfathomable. I mean sure, I'm rich, and some might consider me good looking, but they were all perfectly normal during the interview process. I'd had hope for each and every one of them, but somewhere around the one month mark, things always went sideways.

They dressed a little sexier, showing off more skin in outfits highly inappropriate for spending time with a four year old girl. They stuck around for dinner, and issued more invitations for more activities with daddy and daughter. Month after month, for the past six months, it was the same damn thing.

Nanny trying to kiss me.

Nanny showing her tits.

Nanny naked in my bed.

Nanny offering me a blow job.

If I were a different man I might have taken a few of

them up on what they were offering, but I had no plans to shell out money for sexual harassment lawsuits when I had no problem finding a woman to warm my bed when I wanted one. It wasn't my style to mix business with pleasure, and after the way things had gone with my ex-wife, I needed my home to be stable and conflict free. For me and for Lena.

I broke down and called the nanny agency my assistant had recommended months ago. "Elite Nanny Service, how may I assist you today?"

My shoulders relaxed at the woman's professional, cheery tone. "I'm in need of a nanny as fast as you can send one."

There was a beat of silence and then a different woman's voice sounded in my ear. "Hello. This is Serenity Majors, with whom am I speaking?"

"My name is Dante Rush, and I need a nanny for my four year old daughter, Lena."

"Mr. Rush," she sighed. "I'm a big fan of your fashion."

"You know who I am, that's good. It means you know I'm serious about this, and that I need a nanny immediately."

"Yes, I'm aware of who you are, so we can skip the part where I tell you that my nannies are all professionals with degrees and years of experience, and as such, expect to be compensated appropriately for their services."

"I assure you I plan to pay above minimum wage. When will she be available to start?" I sounded like a grumpy asshole and I knew it, but I was already over this day even though it was just after noon.

Serenity laughed, the sound soft and musical, easy on the ears, even if I didn't know what the hell was so damn funny. "It doesn't work that way, Mr. Rush."

"Well how *does* it work Ms. Majors?"

She sighed, like I was some child she had to explain things to slowly. "How did you last agency match you?"

I frowned. "I've never used a nanny, ah, agency before."

She gasped. "A man with your wealth and looks? Please tell me you didn't put an ad in the paper or online."

I frowned inside my car. "Okay, I won't tell you that."

This time Serenity laughed loudly, and for far too long for a professional phone call. "All right Mr. Rush. There's a certain science to matching a family with the right nanny, and that starts with a questionnaire. Normally parents come to the office and fill it out, but I'm assuming by your tone that you're too busy for such a detour?"

"That would be a correct assumption."

"All right. Do you have the time now?"

Now? "If it means you'll send a nanny immediately, then sure."

Ms. Majors started with basic questions about my work hours, marital status and yearly earnings before she moved on to questions about Lena, her likes and dislikes.

"Is she an active little girl?"

"Why does that matter?"

"The same reason it matters that you make high end,

designer clothing for women of all ages and sizes." At my silence she sighed. "Because I have quite a few older nannies who do well with indoor kids, those who like to spend their time drawing, playing video games and things like that."

"Oh." There it was again, that feeling that I was an asshole. "Lena is both. She loves to play with her dolls and stuffed animals, but she also loves to be outside."

"Will Lena require any educational time during her days?"

"I would really appreciate that," I said in an effort to sound more accommodating.

She asked what felt like about one thousand questions before we were finished. "Thank you for your time and patience, Mr. Rush. I will get back with you soon with a match or two. Will you make yourself available to interview the prospective nannies?"

"Yes," I grunted. "Just be sure she's competent and won't try to worm her way into my bed."

"Noted," she said with a hint of amusement. "And you make sure you don't prey on a pretty young nanny who's reliant on you for a pay check." Before I could defend myself, Serenity ended the call.

"Damn!" I smacked the steering wheel and stepped from the SUV. I waved at Billie who was packing up her van parked on the driveway.

"Hey Billie, thanks so much for staying until I could get home."

"No worries Dante, I know how hard it is to find good

childcare when you're a working single parent." Billie was a single mom to a seven year old son herself. Little Jeremy often accompanied his mom on her jobs on the weekends, and sometimes after school. "Lena's fine, just looked in on her, she's playing and doesn't seem to be upset."

After Billie drove off, I took a rare moment to let the Texas sun beat down on my face before I stepped inside the sprawling ranch style mansion that I had moved into after my divorce.

"Lena?" There was nothing but silence, but a beat later I smiled at the sound of Lena's tiny feet smacking against the tiled floor just outside her playroom.

"Daddy!" She rushed towards me and I bent to scoop her in my arms. "You're home!"

"I am. How are you?"

Lena shrugged, her big blue eyes darted left and right. "I'm good Daddy." She sighed. "Lisa is gone."

I hugged my girl tighter. "I know honey but I'm working on getting you a nanny who will stick. I promise."

"You can stay home?" There was such hope in her eyes.

"I can for a while, but sometimes I'm needed at the office Lena. You know that." I barely had any time in my day for anything but the necessities, but I made sure we ate dinner together most nights. Still, I felt like I was failing in the fatherhood department.

"I know Daddy." She sighed and her tone was so sad it was like someone had punched me in the heart.

"How about after I check a few emails, we go out for lunch? Your choice."

Her eyes and smile both widen with excitement. "Okay Daddy. Promise?"

I nodded, hating that she needed a promise to believe me, but running a fashion empire was more than a full-time job, and there were many times in her short life that I had to break a promise.

"I promise Lena. One hour."

"Okay." She squirmed out of my arms and I lowered her to the floor. "One hour!" Lena ran off back to her playroom.

I followed her down the hall at a far more sedate pace and went to my home office to get sixty minutes—no more — of work of done before spending time with my kid.

Hopefully Ms. Majors would call with good news before the day was over.

Chapter 3

Lucy

"Sorry about the wait Lucy." Serenity sighed and tossed her stylish green framed glasses on her petite glass desk. "Thanks for sticking around."

I shrugged and kept a smile on my face because I liked Serenity, she was a good employer and made sure we received good wages. "Not like I have anything else to do." I kept my tone lighthearted, so she'd know I understood she was doing what she could to find me a placement.

"That's what took so long," she explained. "I had a family all lined up for you, and you can still interview with them, but I received a call not too long ago from a very frantic father in need of a nanny immediately. I actually think you might be a better match for this family."

A frantic father. "A single father?" I didn't have a problem with single fathers in general, but those who used this service could be hit or miss.

"Yes. But don't worry, one of his main requirements

was that you don't try to, and I quote, '*worm your way into his bed.*' So," she sighed and flashed a friendly smile, "you can see why I thought you might be perfect."

I felt my face heat with embarrassment at the reminder of my first year with Elite Nanny Service. "I'm much better now," I said defensively. "But I do admit that there might be a hint of bias where wealthy single dads are concerned." Seriously, how hard was it for a rich, moderately good looking man to find a woman to warm his bed? "And the child?"

"A four year old little girl who is reading at an eight year old level. Loves princesses, unicorns and watching the cloud shapes roll by. Some educational games are required, and it's full-time. Live-in." Serenity watched me carefully, and I made sure to keep my expression blank while I mulled it over.

"You think this is a better fit than the original family?"

"I do, but the choice is yours." Her lips twitched and I arched a suspicious brow across the desk.

"What?"

"He's offering a fifty percent pay bump, permanent, if you can start before the end of the week."

My eyes widen at that juicy morsel. "Really?"

Serenity nodded.

I wanted to jump on this opportunity, to grab it with both hands, but experience had told me to look all gift horses in the mouth. "What's the catch?"

She sighed, but her smile never wavered. "Caught that, did you?"

I nodded and folded my arms, the salary bump all but vanishing before my eyes. "What is it?"

"He's, well... let's just say grumpy and leave it at that."

Grumpy? "I can handle that, since hopefully I won't have to interact with him that much right?"

"That's exactly what I knew our resident optimist would say. Everyone seems grumpy next to you, so I doubt you'll notice anything except your growing bank account."

"Fair point. When's the interview?"

"He wants you to start ASAP. I'll send you a message after I contact the Dad. Just please, don't dress sexy."

My head fell back and laughter spilled out of me. "I doubt I even have any clothes that any person would consider sexy." I haven't been on a date in more than two years, and that was just fine with me.

"With those curves most things look sexy on you," Serenity said sincerely.

"Thanks, but my last date told me, on our first date, that I'd be pretty if I lost a little weight."

Serenity's eyes widened in horror. "He didn't!"

"He did. And I've spent too many of my twenty-five years hating my body and wishing for something unattainable, which God gave my beauty queen older sister in spades." My shoulders sagged at the mention of my older sister, and my parents who practically worshipped her. "Anyway, no worries about me dressing sexy. I'll have on a different version of this," I motioned to my jeans and t-shirt.

"I said don't dress sexy on the job, but you're still young, and too young to give up on love."

I arched a brow at her well meaning advice. "How old were you when you gave up?"

"Point taken," she said around a smile. "But you still have everything it takes to be a good partner and parent with the right man. It would be a waste of all your sunshine not to share it."

"I haven't given up," I finally admitted. "But when the right man comes along, he won't mind my curves, casual clothes or my optimism. Until then, I'm focused on my career." And this pay bump might allow me to save enough to start my life by buying a small house, then I could accept full-time nanny assignments that don't require me to live on site.

"That works out well for me, and I plan to take full advantage of it." She set the tablet containing the family's information on the desk and sighed. "I'll hold off on the other family until after your interview with Grumpy Dad. Their nanny is leaving in two weeks, so they're more flexible."

I laughed. "Is that what we're calling him?"

"Not to his face," she said with a wink and a conspiratorial smile.

"Thanks, Serenity." I tried not to get my hopes up, but the truth was, I was already tallying up my savings after one year on the job.

Chapter 4

Dante

"**L**isten Ricardo. I've heard you out, and now it's your turn to listen. Under no circumstances are you going to add one of your boy toy's designs to *my* clothing line. Tell me you understand." I pinched the bridge of my nose and clenched my jaws to avoid blowing up at my creative director. The man was the best at what he did, putting out ads that increased sales and drew attention to the brand. But right now he was getting on my nerves.

"I understand Dante and you know I love you, but just consider it. Sven isn't just a boy toy, he's a talented designer. I sent you his portfolio, so please, look for yourself. Gotta go. Toodles."

The call ended, and though I was grateful it was over, his abrupt ending pissed me off after he spent fifteen minutes begging for something I wasn't inclined to give. My temples throbbed, I rubbed them in small circles and silently begged the pain to go away. I didn't have time for a headache.

As if to taunt me, the doorbell chose that moment to ring and my eyes fell shut. There was never a moment of peace or quiet, never a down moment to just relax with nothing to do. The bell sounded again and I groaned.

"Dotty!" The housekeeper had been doing double, okay triple duty lately, and I knew I was putting too much on her, but the stupid doorbell was about to drive me mad.

Dotty didn't answer, and when the bell rang for a third time, I shoved out of my office chair and marched to the front door, ready to unleash my frustration on whomever stood at my doorstep. I yanked the door open with so much force it smacked against the frame and bounced back. "What in...what are *you* doing here?"

A pair of familiar blue eyes and long, golden blond hair met me and her smile slowly faded into something that looked like contempt, but it disappeared quickly. Too quickly to be genuine.

"You're Mr. Rush?"

My lips curled into a smile. "Here for your payday? Well you can forget about that. No matter how you try to twist things so that the accident was my fault, no insurance company or court will make me give you one dime." I glared at her, feeling furious that last night's jerk off to the memory of this woman with the smart mouth was the last I'd have, because I simply didn't do gold diggers, money grabbers or whatever else they're called these days.

She nodded, her long hair bounced slightly around her

shoulders. "That's a cool speech, did you practice it in a mirror or something?"

My gaze narrowed. How was she able to get under my skin and my collar at the same time? And why was she still smiling? "Excuse me?"

"That speech, it was pretty good. Did you practice it?"

I closed my eyes and inhaled deeply, exhaling even slower until every angry breath was gone before I opened my eyes. "What are you doing here?"

She sighed. "I'm trying to find out if you're Dante Rush so that I'll know if I'm in the right place."

"You're not here about the accident?"

Her face was lit with annoyance, which made her look like an adorable angry mouse. It was the least frightening thing I could think of. "Are you, or are you not, Dante Rush?"

"I am." I would play along with this charade, but only because I was curious where she would take it. "What can I do for you?"

She sighed and cranked her smile up just a little more. "This is unfortunate, but I'm Lucy Lions, and I'm here to interview for the nanny placement." Her tone was confident and even, gone was any trepidation.

I watched her closely for a long moment and took stock of everything from the long blond hair that reached her elbows, big blue eyes that were almost too big for her delicate face. She had a tiny button nose, lips that bordered on too full. Her soft, sun-kissed skin said she was a woman who spent a lot of time under the Texas sun. I couldn't help the direction my thoughts took when my gaze dropped lower, and took in the soft pink t-shirt she wore and the near painted on jeans that showed off less curves than yesterday, but still enough to make a man's blood pressure skyrocket. Hot pink sneakers completed her look. It didn't seem like she was trying to look sexy, but she had unfortunately achieved it all the same.

"*You're* the nanny?"

She nodded slowly. "I am a nanny yes, whether I'm the nanny for your daughter remains to be seen." There was a challenge in her gaze, in the tilt of her chin as if she knew I was ready to send her away.

"Come in." I stepped back, but she didn't advance. "What now?"

"I'm just trying to figure you out. Is the nanny position still on the table as of right now?"

I appreciated her tough stance, her courage. But I wouldn't give her the satisfaction of knowing that I was desperate for help. I couldn't.

"Only one way to find out." Indecision showed on her face before she stepped inside and handed me a copy of her resumé. "Tell me about Lena."

I frowned. "I'm the one doing the interviewing, Ms. Lions."

"So am I," she shot back with a saucy smile. "We both get to decide if this arrangement will work for us. I can overlook your actions, provided I feel that I can provide your daughter with what she needs."

"You can overlook *my* actions? The traffic incident, you mean?"

She shrugged. "Is there something else you did that I should know about?" Her lips twitched, and it was all I could do not to kick her out on her round ass. Her very lucious, round ass. "So, Lena?"

I glanced at her resume and saw that she was qualified with a master's degree in addition to years of experience, even a couple years teaching kindergarten. She had innovative ideas for children with learning difficulties as well as gifted children.

"Impressive."

"Right?" She laughed when I looked up at her, and I wondered if anything could wipe that smile off her face.

"Follow me." I figured that inside my office, the desk would provide both a physical and figurative barrier between us, which would hopefully make it easier to conduct a professional interview.

"Of course," she mumbled as she stepped inside the office.

"What?" My brows dipped into a frown at those two little words, so filled with derision. "You find something wrong with my office?"

"Not at all," she answered with a smile. "I'm actually not at all surprised that this is what your office looks like. So, tell me about Lena."

"Don't corral me, Ms. Lions."

She shrugged. "It's a habit born from spending too much time with children."

I sighed, refusing to touch that attempt to goad me. "Lena is great. She's bright and bubbly, but she's also headstrong and determined to be the boss of her life."

Her smile was beautiful as she listened. "Pushing boundaries. It's to be expected, but nothing behavioral I presume?"

"No. Not even a fight over bedtime. Most nights."

Lucy nodded. "Are there any particular subjects you want Lena to learn or skills to improve?"

"Good question. She's a great reader, and I guess it's too soon for math or science, so what I would like, is for her nanny to let her help with tasks that will teach her practical things, and encourage games that will do the same." None of the other previous nannies had asked these types of questions, and I began to feel hopeful.

"Do you have a chef?"

My brows dipped. "Excuse me?"

Lucy smiled again. "I'm just wondering if there's someone who might throw a fit if Lena and I were to make cookies or dinner. Cooking is an excellent way to teach basic math through counting and measuring, plus science."

"Science? Really?"

"Baking is chemistry. Too much baking soda in cookies and you'll have puffy, bitter cookies. Too much butter and they will spread too much and become globs instead of golden and crunchy. Science."

Interesting. "Congratulations Ms. Lions you're still in

the running." I stood from my seat and she mimicked my moves.

"So are you, Mr. Rush." She laughed when I froze and glared at her. "Put that scowl away please, it doesn't scare me. Are we off to meet Lena now?"

I nodded. "My scowl scares everybody," I growled at her.

"I'm sure that at whatever high powered job you hold, people tremor when they see you coming. To me, you're just a dad."

I frowned. *Whatever high powered job you hold.* Did she not know who I was? Did I care? Not really. It was refreshing to be around a woman who spoke her mind and didn't bend over backwards to please me. *Even though I wouldn't mind bending her over backwards.* Enough!

"Lena, sweetheart, can you come into the sitting room please?"

"Coming Daddy!"

Chapter 5

Lucy

Holy hell, Dante Rush was even hotter when I wasn't annoyed with him.

Okay, I was still annoyed with him, because seriously, who answered the door the way he did? The man was as rude and ornery as he was sinfully hot. Instead of the expensive suit, he was dressed casually in black jeans that hugged muscular thighs, and a mint green shirt that made his green eyes more intense. Today his hair wasn't mussed from frustrated hands, instead it was perfectly styled, short on the sides with longer waves on top. The green shirt stretched across a broad chest and highlighted corded biceps.

Damn, but the man was gorgeous from head to toe, unfortunately, he was also rude.

"Who is caring for Lena while you're in between nannies?"

My question interrupted his scowling, which only

intensified his frown. "My housekeeper Dotty. She's been here since Lena was a baby. Why?"

"Just curious." I shrugged off his grunted question with a smile.

"Dotty is perfectly capable of look after her, she's raised four children of her own.

"I have no doubt, Mr. Rush. It was just a question."

"Didn't feel like *just a question*," he mumbled under his breath, but loud enough for me to hear.

A laugh bubbled out of me unconsciously. He was as hot as he was irritable, and was he ever irritable!

"Something funny, Ms. Lions?" His black brows dipped into a furious vee.

"Apparently I find you amusing."

Small footsteps grew closer and closer until a little girl appeared with big blue eyes and wavy black hair just like her father's. Her hair was twisted into adorable pigtails with a tiara perched on top. She came to an abrupt stop and smiled, clasping her hands behind her back and rocking on her heels. "Are you a princess?"

"Me?" I laughed lightly and shook my head. "Sadly I am not a princess, if so, I might have a fancy tiara just like yours."

As if she'd forgotten about it, Lena touched the sparkly tiara and giggled. "I love princesses. And unicorns."

"Me too," I offered with a smile. "I'm Lucy, and I love unicorns because they fart glitter." She giggled again and I leaned forward and whispered, "And my dream is to become a unicorn princess."

Her blue eyes widened prettily and she gasped. "Me too!"

I held a hand out and she put her hand in mine and very politely introduced herself. "I'm Lena, nice to meet you."

"It's very nice to meet you Lena."

She grinned and turned to face her father, whose expression had softened when he looked at his daughter. She scrambled around the desk and climbed into his lap to wrap her arms around him. It was nice to get a glimpse of the marshmallow underneath the hard grumpy exterior when he interacted with Lena. He held her gently in his strong arms, like she was the most precious of cargo.

"Lena, Lucy wants to be your new nanny."

"Okay! Yes, please."

I laughed at her excitement. "I hear that you like to read?"

She gave an exaggerated nod. "I love it. Animals and princesses and even outer space books."

"I'll have to keep that in mind if I'm invited back." It was best not to get the kids' hopes up, because parents were often the fickle ones. Especially Dante Rush. "It was nice to meet you Lena."

"It was nice to meet you Lucy." She smacked a loud kiss to her dad's cheek, scrambled down and rushed out in a blur.

"If I could bottle that energy..." I began with a laugh.

Dante surprised me by joining in with a deep, rumbling laugh of his own. It was so unexpected, my eyes widened at how even more beautiful he was when he laughed. "I tell myself that at least once a day."

I gave myself another long moment to just enjoy his beauty before I gave myself a mental slap to stop ogling the man who might be my boss in a few minutes. "So, anything else you want to tell me about Lena? Special diet? Or anything else you can think of?"

"Nothing like that. She has a mean sweet tooth that I indulge far too often." He flashed another smile that was so hot I pushed my knees together to stop the pulsing between my thighs.

"Noted. One more thing, Serenity mentioned you were divorced, but she didn't say if Lena's mom was involved."

All traces of the smile vanished immediately, replaced by a darker version of his trademark scowl. "There will be no crossing of professional boundaries, Ms. Lions. If I decide to hire you."

I rolled my eyes and sighed with frustration. This interview was more adventurous than a roller coaster. But because I knew it would piss him off, I sat taller and I smiled. "Good to know Mr. Rush, but I was curious because sometimes there are complicated custody and visitations issues between divorced couples. It's easier to navigate if I know what to expect."

His expression would have been comical if he wasn't so insulting before. "Okay then. Her mother Bethany lives in Spain with her new husband. As far as I'm aware, she hasn't been back to the United States since our divorce was finalized." His jaw clenched, and that was his only show of emotion, but it made me wonder if it was really over with the ex-wife he might still love, or if the fact that she'd so easily abandoned her daughter was the source of his rage. "Bethany's parents call once a week, but it's usually on the weekends and I can be around to supervise. My parents," he sighed. "They love Lena and they call often, video chats," he groaned. "But they live in Florida so you don't have to worry about unexpected visits."

I nodded at his reluctant explanation. "That wasn't so hard, was it?"

His jaw clenched again, so hard I thought he might crack a tooth, and his nostrils flared like an angry bull. "Do you want this position or not?"

"Lena seems like a lovely little girl, and I would love to help her discover the world, but ultimately the choice is yours Mr. Rush. I have a few other families I haven't interviewed with yet, so it's best if you let me know as soon as possible."

He wasn't satisfied with my answer, and those green eyes watched me for so long that I had to resist the urge to squirm as I stared back. "Are you always this insubordinate?"

I had to laugh at his pained expression, because I was sure a man like him wasn't used to people talking back or questioning him. "I am almost never insubordinate, but at this exact moment in time, you're not an authority figure, and therefore not someone I need to obey."

His gaze narrowed another fraction, and I knew I

might have pushed him too far. I watched those green eyes and wondered what was going on behind them, because clearly his gears were churning hard. Finally Dante sat back and pressed his fingertips together in that stereotypical powerful businessman way. "You will have to drive the Escalade when you're on the clock. I won't have Lena going around in your tin box."

I sniffed. "My car is two years old, Mr. Rush. It's hardly a tin box." I sat back, nearly mirroring his position. "That seems like a lot of car for two people, but sure. Whatever works for you." I gave him my best sickly sweet smile until his demeanor broke and he rolled he sighed.

"That's what I like to hear." He smiled, but it was more of a grimace. "This is a live-in position, will you need to make arrangements before you can move in?"

"No," I sighed and stood when he did. "My last position ended abruptly when the mother received a promotion on the east coast, so I've been rooming with a friend. When do you need me to start?" It would be maddening to work for this man, but Lena was great and her father was good eye candy. Good, grumpy eye candy.

Dante bent his big body over the table and quickly scribbled on a black sticky note before he handed it to me. "This is the salary if you can start tomorrow."

I looked down, and it was even more than Serenity had said it would be, by a lot. "Are you sure this is the right number?"

He smiled. "I don't make mistakes when it comes to money Ms. Lions."

Damn if those words didn't send a shiver down my spine. "Okay then. I accept your informal offer."

"Excellent," he grunted. "Your room is this way."

"Wait, so that's it? You've decided to hire me?"

His dark brows furrowed. "Is there a reason I shouldn't?"

"Obviously not, I'm great. But Serenity mentioned you'd been doing some week, and month-long auditions in the past."

"That was my habit, yes, but not necessary in this instance. I find you adequate."

"Wow, adequate? Wait until I call up the folks back at home to tell them some fancy businessman finds me adequate. All of my lifelong dreams have come true."

He glared at me with a gaze so cold it probably terrified most people.

I giggled. "So about that room?"

He nodded and turned away, which was a gift from the heavens because his long legs, firm bottom and broad back was the perfect view.

At least until I caught sight of the hotel suite of a room that he showed me. The room was gorgeous, with a large bed that had a fancy, nearly six foot tall decorative headboard. The wood was all blond, cherry or pine, I didn't really know, but it was stunning. Plush carpet under my sneakers, and a view of the well-kept wilderness out the back windows stole my breath.

"Wow," I whispered, and then turned to Dante with a

toothy smile. "Thank you Mr. Rush. I find this room exceptionally adequate."

His lips pursed as if he wanted to say something, but he reconsidered and shook his head.

I laughed again. "I'll see you tomorrow then. Does seven work for you?"

He nodded.

"Okay. Serenity has all the paperwork you'll need to get everything started. When that's done, she'll make it all official."

"Perfect," he grunted.

Yes you are. "Good night, Mr. Rush."

"Dante," he barked. "My name is Dante."

I waved as I hurried past him out of my new bedroom towards the front door. "Have a good one then, *Dante.*"

Chapter 6

Dante

"No Alex, you don't get it. She's like sunshine and sass rolled into one too tempting package." I paced the length of my office and ran a hand through my hair while I spoke to one of my closest friends, Alex Witter, on speakerphone. "It's goddamn frustrating." I shook my head and released a frustrated sigh at the thought of Lucy coming to work and live in my house.

Alex cackled over the call. "Sounds great. I take it she's hot too?"

I sighed and thought about that long blond hair and those big blue eyes. "Is that all you think about? Don't the NFL groupies keep you busy enough?" Alex was the leading running back in the league, and I was sure he had women throwing themselves at him everywhere he went.

"Let me tell you something Dante, a man can never be too busy where beautiful women are concerned. Now tell me, how hot is she?"

"What does that matter?" She was beautiful, but that was irrelevant because she was so damn annoying.

Alex sighed like he was exhausted. "Man you're utterly hopeless, you know that don't you?"

"Fine," I growled and turned on my heels to keep pacing. "She's hot as fuck with long blond hair and curves that just make you want to reach out and fucking touch her! Is that what you want to hear?"

Alex howled with laughter. "That's what I'm talking about! So she's hot *and* she's gonna be living with you, what is the problem exactly?"

"The problem," I whispered and continued to pace, "is that she is like a real life fucking cheerleader. Always so happy and upbeat. Look up chipper in the dictionary, and her face will be right there with pompons. What the hell is there to be so chipper about?"

Instead of answering my question, Alex just chuckled. It was annoying.

"What the hell is so funny?"

"You!" He laughed again, this time so loud I started feeling embarrassed. "You like her," he accused.

"I do not," I shook my head even though he couldn't see me and stopped pacing. "I don't even know her to like or dislike her, and it doesn't matter how I feel, as long as Lena likes her." That's what I kept telling myself, and I would keep on telling myself that until it became true.

"Maybe you don't know her all that well, but I've known you long enough to know that you definitely like her." His smug voice grated on my nerves, but he did know me well to be honest.

"Whatever," I growled. "She's annoying, but more importantly, she's here to look after Lena, not me." The fact that I spent too much of last night thinking of ways she could look after me was my business and mine alone.

"Well if you're not interested, tell me more about this sexy little Mary Poppins, because I might be interested. I know how to handle a woman with a smart mouth." I cringed at the thought of Alex, playboy extraordinaire, seducing my nanny. Lena's nanny that is.

"She's not your type," I growled. "Trust me."

"Just because you find me hideous and undatable doesn't mean all men will, Mr. Rush. And I'll thank you not to talk smack about me to your friends."

Shit. I turned slowly, the sound of Alex's laughter ranging in my ears, until my gaze landed on Lucy's blue eyes. "Lucy."

"Oh shit brother, you're in trouble now," Alex said around loud, guffawing laughter.

"Shut up, Alex."

"Don't be mad at me. Just tell her that you want her and can't think straight. Women love that shit."

"Shut. Up." I growled into the phone while Lucy watched with narrowed eyes and barely concealed laughter on her lips. Lush, full lips. "Lucy," I began again.

Before I could utter even two words, she held up a hand to stop me, a sweet smile on her face. "I just came to let you know that Lena and I are going to the children's history museum. They have an exhibit on royals. That's all." One brow arched, daring me to say anything unrelated to the museum.

"Lena will love that. Take the Escalade."

For the first time there was a flash of temper in her eyes, but ever the professional, she banked it quickly and hit me with an icy stare. "That was part of the agreed upon job conditions," she offered sarcastically, girl next door smile still in place.

"Lucy," I began again and took a step forward.

The stubborn woman twirled on her heels and gave me her back instead of a moment of her time. "Lena, are you ready to go see princesses?"

"Yay! And queens?"

"And queens," she responded with a smile. "Let's hop into our carriage Princess!"

The sound of Lena's sweet giggles was the last thing I heard, but when I pressed my face against the window, there they were, hand in hand as they skipped across the driveway and into the pearl white Escalade.

"Dammit Alex," I growled. "You made me piss off the nanny."

"The good news is that I have a few ideas how you can make her feel better."

My only response was a low growl, because Alex didn't understand. "When you have kids you'll understand." The last thing I wanted was for the nanny to quit because I pissed her off.

Chapter 7

Lucy

Dante Rush was annoying. And stupid.

And gorgeous as all get out.

Damn him, thinking that I was so hideous that not even his friend would find me attractive. Well, you know what? Screw him! No, not screw him. Forget him, at least as much as was possible while living under the same roof. I was comfortable in my own skin, thank you very much. These curves were as much a part of me as the thick blond hair I couldn't bring myself to cut, and my blue eyes that sat a little too far apart.

"Jerk face bastard," I growled as I got dressed for my second day on the job. Yesterday with Lena was just perfect. The little girl *oohed* and *aahed* over the exhibit on royals, soaking up every ounce of information like her life depended on it. I snapped a few dozen photos of her, which I would share with Dante. Eventually.

Today I was going to make him eat his words by

showing him that I was more than just cute, as my mom always referred to me. Without dressing in some skintight miniskirt and sky high heels, I would make Dante regret talking badly about me to his stupid friend.

I dressed carefully in my standard nanny uniform, but with a twist. My favorite pair of dark stretchy pants that molded to my every curve and accentuated my hourglass shape. I chose a deep blue shirt that made my eyes pop, and then I lined them with a smoky brown pencil. And sure, I might have worn a bra that made my D-cups hang nice and perky just to torture him a little, but you know what they say about a woman scorned and all that.

Blue sneakers completed the look with matching blue hair combs that made me look like a combination of the girl next door and a wet dream. "Perfect."

I made my way to Lena's room to find the little girl bouncing with energy on her bed. "Morning Lucy!"

"Good morning, Princess Lena. Did you sleep well?" In the short time I've spent with her, she'd proven to be smart and inquisitive, and so adorable it was hard not to pinch her cheeks all the time.

Lena nodded. "I slept like a princess." She giggled and stopped jumping on her bed. "Clothes?"

I nodded. "Very good. Pick out something and we'll talk about it." I loved watching kids as they learned how to become independent, starting with the clothes they chose to wear. Some kids would wear costumes every day if they were allowed, while others had a hard time matching up prints.

39

"I get to pick?"

I nodded. "You have to wear them, not me. Just make it something you wouldn't mind wearing in public."

Her blue eyes sparkled and then she took off to a closet most grown women would envy, mumbling to herself as she chose. I was tempted to follow her, but I wanted to give her the autonomy to choose without my input.

"Okay Lucy." She ran back from the closet and held up a denim skirt with leggings, and a sparkling tank top with a dancing unicorn on the front.

I couldn't help but smile. "Perfect. Let me help you get dressed and then we'll find some shoes, okay?"

She nodded, and fifteen minutes later we made our way downstairs to the kitchen. Lena chatted the entire time with occasional giggles thrown in, which made it hard to believe she came from the same genes as her grumpy father.

"Morning Daddy!" She sang the words as she released my hand and climbed up the high back stool pushed up against the countertop.

Dante leaned to the side and she pressed a kiss to his cheek. "Morning, honey. Sleep well?"

She nodded and then launched into a highly detailed rundown of our visit to the museum. She talked about the coronation gowns, the different colors worn and why. And of course, the ladies in waiting. "It was the best, Daddy. The best!"

Dante listened to every word she said with a smile,

even interrupting to ask questions. He was an attentive parent, with a lot of love for his little girl.

"Sounds like you had a good time."

"It was so much fun, Daddy. You have to see it."

"Maybe you can show me one of these weekends." He gave her ponytail a playful tug and she giggled before she dug into the breakfast Dotty set in front of her. While she ate, Dante turned to me with a smile. "You could not have found a more perfect activity for her." His broad smile was gorgeous, but I wasn't ready to forgive him.

I shrugged and flashed him my best southern hospitality smile. "Well, I *am* adequate at my job." I smirked at him before I turned on my heels and fled the kitchen.

"Dammit," he muttered under his breath and that only made my smile bigger.

Some days were all about the small victories.

Chapter 8

Dante

I needed to apologize to the nanny. That was my first thought as I came to a stop in the driveway behind the Escalade. Though why I even cared so much was a mystery to me. Lucy worked for me, not the other way around, and despite her snarky yet also chipper attitude, I couldn't stop thinking about her. Three days had passed since she twirled away from my attempt to apologize, and every day since she had been mysteriously absent unless Lena was also around as our unofficial chaperone.

The more I thought about it though, I thought maybe *not* apologizing was the way to go. As long as she was a little annoyed with me, we could keep a professional distance between us that would prevent us both from doing something stupid, like give in to temptation. Like strip every stitch of clothing from her luscious body and make her mine. Only for a night though, because I didn't do long-term, not anymore. No more marriages and no more babies for me. One night, or maybe a few weeks of carnal bliss was all I needed to keep me going.

In the end though, for the sake of keeping the peace, I decided to apologize. I found Lucy and Lena in the backyard. But instead of skipping around the grass or having a tea party, they were laid out on a pink blanket with their heads together facing the sky.

"I see a bunny rabbit!" Lena's excited words stopped my progress across the lawn, and I watched the two females as I rolled up my sleeves and popped the top buttons on my shirt. Lena giggled and pointed at the sky.

"I can't quite see it," Lucy said in a gentle, guiding voice. "How many clouds is this bunny rabbit?"

Without missing a beat, Lena pointed as she counted them out carefully. "See?"

Lucy gasped and nodded. "Oh yeah, now I see it perfectly. Very good, Lena." She was so good at this, finding ways to encourage Lena while infusing even fun activities with learning. "Okay, my turn. I see a pig!" She pointed and did a terrible impression of a pig's oink.

Lena giggled wildly and pointed to the sky once again. "I see it too!" She counted once again, this time without being prompted. "You're good at this game Lucy."

She huffed a laugh and shrugged. "I played this game a lot when I was a little girl, and even during study breaks when I was in college." There was a wistfulness in her voice that sent a multitude of questions firing off inside my head.

Lena gasped. "You played this as a grownup?"

"Yup, I did." There was laughter in Lucy's voice when she answered.

"Not with a little kid like me?"

"Nope. Just with myself. It's soothing, which means calming. You'll see when you start school, sometimes you just need a break, and this was mine."

"I'm always gonna look at the cloud animals!"

Lucy laughed. "You should. You're never too old to take a few moments for yourself."

Damn if there wasn't something totally appealing about the way she spoke to my little girl. Lucy had a knack for talking to kids on their level without it sounding like she was talking down to them. It was clear why she was a sought after nanny, which meant I really, really needed to apologize. I crossed the yard and stood beside them, my body cast a shadow over their smiling faces.

"Excuse me, ladies."

"Hi Daddy!"

I couldn't help but smile at Lena. Every single day, without fail, she greeted me with the kind of excitement only a kid could produce. "Hey sweetheart. Having a good day?"

"The best day, Daddy. You wanna look at cloud animals with us?"

My lips quirked and I ran a hand through my hair. "Maybe. I was hoping to have a word with Lucy, first."

"We're not done yet Daddy."

"She's right," Lucy smirked and shielded her eyes. "If

you want to talk, get down here and find a cloud animal." There was so much laughter in those blue slits, challenging me, that I had no choice but to lie down.

I found a spot right between them, but my body faced the opposite direction because there wasn't enough room the other way. I turned my gaze to the clouds and frowned. "What am I supposed to see exactly?"

Lucy chuckled as her gaze swung to mine. "Use your imagination," she whispered, and that's when I realized what a big mistake I'd made. I should have taken the spot on the other side of Lena because we were so close, her minty breath fanned across my face.

"I save my imagination for more important things." The innuendo in my words made her smile even broader.

A single blond brow arched and she leaned just a little closer. "Try harder."

And now I was thinking about her plump lips tackling something else hard. *Shit.* "How?"

"Pretend this is important to you," she said with a smile, but the fire in her eyes told me she thought I was falling down on the job, and I hated that she was right.

I couldn't resist the challenge she presented, both in physical terms as well as her challenging my parenting. I turned back to the sky and stared at the clouds while they cantered over me.

"I got it! Right there I see a giraffe." I hoped like hell it was a giraffe anyway. I pointed at it as Lena and Lucy leaned closer to follow the path of my fingers.

Lena patted my arm excitedly. "I see it Daddy! One,

two," she started to count the clouds that made up the giraffe.

I turned to Lucy with a fortifying sigh. "I'm sorry that I hurt your feelings, Lucy. Truly. That wasn't my attention, it's just that Alex is an old friend and he knows how to get under my skin."

She said nothing for a few seconds and finally gave me her blue gaze. "I don't care that you don't find me attractive, Mr. Rush, but that doesn't mean that your words didn't hurt. I accept your apology, but I don't appreciate you talking badly about me behind my back."

I nodded, but the relief I expected didn't come. Her words were right and sincere, but it didn't feel as if she truly forgave me. *She never said she did,* I realized. She accepted my apology, which I learned throughout the three years in my torturous marriage, was not the same thing. "Thank you, Lucy."

She shrugged.

"Join us for dinner?"

"I can't," she said quickly and looked away.

"Hot date?" I don't know why I asked that question. It wasn't my business, it was inappropriate, and worse, it made it seem like I cared about the answer. And I didn't. Not really.

Lucy snorted and a bitter laugh rushed out of her. "You don't believe that," she answered and rolled her eyes. "It's an incredibly hot date, going to Toni's apartment to pack up some things so I don't have to go back and forth as often."

"The woman with you the day you ripped me a new one?"

She smiled and didn't bother denying my phrasing. "Yeah, that's her."

Toni was a girl, not a boyfriend. "How is it that you don't have a place of your own?"

She shrugged. "My last assignment ended abruptly when the mom received a promotion that required them to move. It was also live-in, so Toni let me crash at her place until I found a place of my own, or a new live-in assignment came along."

"So basically I saved you?"

She laughed, and it was throaty and sexy. "If that's what you need to believe, have at it."

I found myself smiling at her constant need to put me in my place. Never met a woman who did that, not even Bethany had done that, unless she really meant it and wanted to hurt me.

"You're free to use the Escalade. It has a lot more room than your sedan."

"Thank you, but the Escalade is my work car, and I am officially," she glanced down at the sleek black band on her left wrist and smiled as she got to her feet, "off the clock."

"I'm your boss, and I'm telling you it's okay to use it." Why was she so stubborn? I got up too, feeling more confident now that I was back on my feet, on equal footing with Lucy.

Her gaze inched up my body, and I took a step back realizing how close I was, and how big our height differ-

47

ence was. I didn't want her to think I was intimidating her on purpose. "I've been doing this for a long time Mr. Rush and I have a system for keeping things professional, but thanks again for the offer." She flashed that smile that made it feel as if she had a secret that only she knew.

"Dante." Why I felt the need to keep reminding her to use my first name I had no idea, though I was sure Alex would have plenty.

"Right. Dante." She took a few steps back, but not before I caught a flare of desire in her eyes.

Interesting. No, it wasn't interesting. It was unfortunate, because neither of us could act on it. "Was that so hard?"

She rolled her eyes. "You have no idea." Her gaze swung to Lena who still counted clouds. "Do you want a progress report now?"

I shook my head and waved her off. "Monday is soon enough. Enjoy your night Lucy."

"Oh yeah, big night of packing and loading up my car." She laughed nervously. "You too...Dante. Bye Lena, see you later."

"Buh bye Lucy!"

She turned and walked across the backyard.

I mentally patted myself on the back for only staring at her ass for a few seconds when I actually really wanted to stare until she disappeared from my view.

Chapter 9

Lucy

"Wow, you ordered from my favorite barbecue place? You must've really missed me." I smiled across the table at Toni as we unpacked the bags of food that smelled so delicious my stomach growled in response.

Toni shrugged, but the blush that stained her pale cheeks told me she had, in fact, missed having me around the apartment. "You haven't called." She didn't look up, and I frowned. Toni was the tough one, but clearly my oversight had hurt her.

"I'm sorry Toni, getting settled has been harder this time around." I knew she would have questions, and since I owed her an apology, I folded them together. "Because I failed to check in with you, I'm going to give you the best gift in the world."

She pulled out the last aluminum container and sat. "Oh yeah? I'm listening."

As we made up our plates and ate, I gave Toni the rundown of my week, starting with the interview. "Imagine my surprise when the door opened and the father turned out to be that gorgeous prick who caused the accident."

"No!" Her wide green eyes filled with the same shock I'd felt in the moment.

"Yep. And it turns out that he's even *more* entitled than I initially thought! Though I suppose that comes with living in a mansion and stuff."

"A mansion, like a real life mansion, or just a big suburban home?"

"No Toni, an actual mansion. It's a big sprawling ranch style mansion, complete with a circle driveway, a small well-kept wooded area just beyond the manicured backyard. It's stunning." It was the perfect playground for an imaginative little girl like Lena.

"How did he react to you showing up on his doorstep?"

I laughed and rolled my eyes, giving her the whole story until she cried with laughter. "He actually thought I was there trying to get money from him for my car."

"Oh wow. You set him straight?"

I nodded. "I did. There's something about him that makes me feel bolder and sassier. I hold my own with him, and I don't' think he's used to that, because he turns his grumpy meter up just for me."

"Yeah, yeah," she waved a dismissive hand. "He's grumpy as all get out, but what I really want to know is, how hot he really is. Was that day on the road just a trick of the light, or was my vision impaired by my hangover that day?"

"I wish!" I groaned and shook my head. "He's even sexier, especially when he smiles. And when he's dressed casually. He does sinful things to a pair of denim." The thought of him in those jeans was enough to fill my mind with dirty thoughts of tugging those jeans off his long legs. "Thankfully he's irritating as heck, or else I might find it hard to stay professional. Well that, and the fact that he thinks I'm hideous."

Which still hurt me like heck. I know not everyone would find me attractive, hell most men didn't, but hearing it said out loud like that stung.

Toni scowled and smacked a fist on the table. "I'll beat his gorgeous face to a pulp Luce, just say the word."

I smiled, filled with gratitude to have a friend like Toni. "I handled it, and he apologized." I would try not to feel too bad that he never actually said he found me attractive, just apologized for hurting my feelings.

Toni grinned. "He probably said that to warn his friend off making a move on you. I saw the way he looked at you that first day, like he wanted to eat you alive."

"You're mistaken," I assured her. "I heard it with my own ears." I shook off thoughts of Dante and his non-attraction to me. "Anyway, enough of my drama, how was your week?"

Toni smiled knowingly, but thankfully she didn't call me out for my obvious and clumsy change of topic. "It was all right. Serenity got me set up with a new assignment, some guy who now has custody of his niece, but I have another week before I report for duty."

"That's good, right?"

She nodded. "Of course. I'm happy, but what am I gonna do for another week?"

"Learn to relax? Go out and do all the things you won't be able to do once you're back on the clock?" Toni didn't actually need the money she made as a nanny, which made it even more surprising that she didn't enjoy being idle.

"Ugh, that's horrible advice," she groaned. "I'll get the house straightened out, so when either of us come back for the weekends, it's not full of dust and dirty dishes." She got up from the table to retrieve beers for both of us. "I'll find a way to keep busy. I just hope the uncle isn't as difficult as your sexy dad, though some eye candy would be nice."

I rolled my eyes. "He's great eye candy until he opens his mouth." I cracked open my beer and raised it for a toast. "Here's hoping that your next boss is better than Dante Rush."

Toni froze at my words and her green eyes went wide in shock. "What did you say?"

"That I hope your next boss is better than mine?"

"Dante Rush?"

"Yeah. You know him or something?" I figured he was some type of businessman, but it never occurred to me he might be famous as well. I suppose I should have cyber stalked him as any responsible woman in this day and age should, but there was just no time.

"Uh yeah, so does the entire world. Dante Rush, as in, House of Rush?" At my blank stare she rolled her eyes and reached for her phone as she explained. " The fashion house that does luxury designer goods as well as fashionable budget brands for regular people. The man is a bona fide bazillionaire."

I frowned. "He's a bona fide thing that doesn't exist? Cool."

Toni growled her frustration. "Do you live under a rock or something?"

"When it comes to fashion, apparently I do." The heat of humiliation stung though. "That jerk-face bastard," I growled. "He knew I had no idea who he was." Dante had mocked me yet again, and I didn't like it one bit. Screw his insincere apology.

"And?"

"And I don't like being made fun of, even if I should be used to it." My sister and her friends did it often enough, and some might say it was a bit of a trigger for me. "Whatever. Doesn't matter."

"Seems to matter," Toni mumbled under her breath. "How about we go out and drink away your sorrows. Or humiliation or whatever."

"Sounds good." A night away from Dante was just what I needed.

Chapter 10

Dante

Lucy didn't come home last night, and I couldn't deny that I was worried. *Or jealous,* my conscience added sarcastically. She had every right to spend the night away from home when she wasn't on the clock. Still, where in the hell was she? I was half-tempted to call her at around ten in the morning, but an unexpected call from Italy took up time until lunch rolled around.

Lena and I ate lunch at the kitchen table where we had most of our meals unless it was a special occasion, and then we used the formal dining room. The door opened and seconds later Lucy appeared looking fresh and young, and too damn good in capri yoga pants that hugged her body nicely and a loose tank top that showed off plump tits. She was dressed perfectly decent, but my mind was clearly in the gutter when it came to Lucy.

"Good afternoon. I just wanted you to know that I was

back." Her smile was wide but it didn't quite reach her eyes.

Everything within me wanted to go to her and ask if she was all right, but Lena rushed from the table and slammed her body against Lucy's legs. "You came back!"

Lucy dropped down, her brows dipped in concern as she wrapped her arms around my daughter. "Of course I came back. We had fun together this week, didn't we?"

Lena nodded. "Lots of fun."

This time her smile was genuine when she pulled back and stared at Lena. "I needed to visit my friend and grab a few of my things to make my room feel like home. Were you worried about me?"

She nodded again and pushed her lip out into a pout. "I thought you were gone forever. Like my mommy."

"Aw, honey." She pulled her in for another hug and the gesture was so motherly I felt a pinch inside my chest. "I'm sorry I worried you. Next time I'll let you know exactly when I'll be back. Okay?"

"Next time? You're going away again?"

She nodded. "I don't work on the weekends, so sometimes I might not be here while you spend time with your dad."

"You could stay with us all the time," she implored. "Want some breakfast?"

"As delicious as it smells, I need to unload my car and get my things sorted in my room. If I have food now, I'll probably find another reason to delay. Finish your breakfast and have fun with your dad, okay?"

Lena nodded. "Okay Lucy. But you can come find us anytime you want. Right Daddy?"

My lips twitched. "Of course, sweetheart."

"Thank you, Lena. That's so thoughtful of you." She rubbed a hand over Lena's hair and left the kitchen.

Having her in the house but out of sight was somehow more distracting than having her gone. I knew she was in my house, upstairs, but she stayed in her room for hours. She didn't emerge even once for a break, which had me reconsidering the small fridge I had Dotty put in the nanny suite.

I didn't know if she was purposely avoiding me, or if she really wanted to give me and Lena family time without distraction, but I wanted to see her. By the time nine o'clock rolled around, I was ready to go upstairs and tell her to stop avoiding me. Lena had been bathed and tucked into bed for nearly an hour and I managed to get some more work done, but my stomach reminded me of my need for food. I headed upstairs to find Lucy and see if I could tempt her into having dinner with me.

When I found her, she still had on those sexy yoga pants, tempting as hell as she finished off a tall glass of water. "She lives."

Lucy smiled as she turned to face me. "Barely. You'd think I moved an entire apartment with how tired I feel." She didn't look exhausted, she looked beautiful and fresh faced. "Where's Lena?"

"Bed." I frowned. "You think I'm so deficient as a parent that she doesn't have a bedtime?"

"Touchy, touchy, Mr. Rush." She glanced at her wrist and frowned. "I just didn't realize it was so late."

Dammit, she was right. I was touchy, but I shrugged it off. "I thought maybe you were avoiding me again." I walked over to her. "I already apologized."

She rolled her eyes and sighed. "And I accepted." She set the glass down and glared up at me. "Whatever you think of me Dante, I don't need every man on the planet to want to get into my pants. Especially these pants," she huffed as she slid her hands up her thighs. "From House of Rush."

I blinked innocently at her peeved tone. "Interesting?"

She laughed and humor lit her eyes so I knew she wasn't too upset, or maybe that was just the hope of a desperate man. "Don't even try it, I'll bet you enjoyed that I didn't know you were a big deal. I'm sure you and your friends had a good laugh at the clueless new nanny."

Her tone sounded truly hurt and I hated that. I didn't talk smack about people except business rivals. "I wouldn't do that Lucy, not ever. It was refreshing to be in a room with someone who didn't know who I was, who didn't kowtow to me. You treat me normal, give as good as you get, and even though it's damned annoying, I like it."

"Better," she shot back with a laugh. "You get better than you give."

I laughed because she seriously never gave an inch, and the more she did it, the more I liked it. "So now that you know who I am, a big deal and all," she rolled her eyes and I laughed. "Does this mean you'll be more obedient?"

I hoped not, but she wouldn't be the first woman, hell the first person to change once she realized that I was the elusive *somebody*.

Lucy laughed even harder as her hand landed on my chest. She patted my chest like a child. "Aw, wouldn't that be great if the answer was yes?"

Ignore it, I told myself regarding her touch, so hot I felt the fire shoot down my spine. "Yes," I managed to grunt in response.

"Yeah, it would," she conceded with a small nod. "But I think I'll keep things as they are."

"I would be disappointed if you didn't." That much was true, then again if she would just step in line maybe my attraction to her would fade. "Have you eaten dinner?" Or maybe I was just a glutton for punishment, trying to spend more time with a woman who tempted me to break my own rules.

"I haven't, but I guess now I will." She glanced at the fridge with low, exhausted shoulders.

"Dotty doesn't work on the weekends, but these fingers do." I wiggled them and heat flared in her eyes. *Interesting*. "For dialing," I clarified with a laugh. "Get your mind out of the gutter Lucy."

She stood taller and jutted her chin out. "I have no idea what you're talking about."

I let that lie go. For now. "Does pizza work for you?"

"Sure, but only if it comes with some super spicy chicken bites and extra ranch dressing."

A woman who enjoyed food was refreshing. "I can do that."

"Then I'm in for dinner. I need to finish up and shower so I'll be back in thirty minutes." She glanced down at her wrist and nodded. "Yeah, thirty minutes."

"So, an hour?" She looked up at me and I arched a brow, daring her to deny it.

Without a word she walked away but she stopped just before entering her bedroom. "Okay fine, an hour."

I went back downstairs, trying like hell not to think of Lucy in the shower.

Chapter 11

Lucy

"You made it in twenty minutes," Dante said with a sexy little smirk as I trotted down the staircase. "Impressive."

"You think so?" I asked the question as I walked through what he called the sitting room and into the kitchen to grab a bottle opener for the craft beers Toni had given me. I handed one to Dante with a wide smile.

"I do. I expected you to at least take longer than thirty minutes." He chuckled and took a long pull from the beer bottle.

I shrugged and dropped down on the plush pale blue sofa. "No need to get all dolled up for anyone, especially when I'm perfectly adequate the way I am." My lips tugged into a teasing smile when he froze.

Dante groaned and smacked a hand to cover his face. "I'm never going to live that down, am I?"

"Nope." I made sure the last syllable popped loudly and gave him my sunniest smile. "Why should I let you?"

"Pity?" Before I could say anything more, the doorbell rang and announced a visitor. "That'll be the food," he said and got off the sofa with a grunt.

I got up from the sofa too and made my way to the kitchen to gather plates and silverware. It was just pizza, but I figured a guy like Dante wouldn't eat it straight from the box.

A moment later Dante met me in the kitchen and nodded towards the French doors. "It's nice out, you feel like eating out back?"

"Sure." The weather was great this time of year and the evenings were mild, perfect for eating outside. I carried the plates and forks outside and set them carefully before I took my seat. "How much do I owe you for dinner?"

That question earned a scowl from Dante. "You think I'll go broke feeding you?"

"No," I rolled my eyes. "Of course not. But I can pay for my own meals since I'm off the clock."

"I told you that you are allowed to eat whatever you want from the kitchen, on or off the clock." His tone was one I was sure worked often on most people in his orbit, but I was a stubborn sort.

"Agreed, but this," I motioned to the boxes on the table, "is not from the kitchen."

He scowled in my direction, his dark glare aimed

squarely at me. "Do you get some sort of life force from arguing with me?"

I laughed and shook my head. "Not at all, but like I said I am perfectly capable of paying my own way, and I don't want you think I'm trying to take advantage of your generosity." Dante's gaze drilled into me, almost down to my soul and I let him look his fill before I dug into the pizza and chicken poppers.

"I appreciate that Lucy, more than you know. Honestly." His gaze was genuine and sincere, and I had a feeling there were too many people in his life who used him for what he had, rather than what he was.

"So how much do I owe?"

He leaned forward with a sexy yet playful grin. "Consider tonight's dinner on me. Can you do that?"

"I'm not sure..." I stammered out. "Why would you pay for my meal?"

"Because having companionship for dinner is worth more than the price of this meal, by a lot." His words were plain and simple, but the sentiment beneath gave me pause.

"Are you lacking for companionship Dante?"

He nodded. "I have a few friends who don't care who I am out in the world. But I don't spend nearly enough time with them due to our busy schedules."

I nodded as if I understood. "Other high powered, entitled dudes?"

He smirked. "Close enough. Though I think they would all bristle at the "entitled" label, as would I."

I laughed. "Are we forgetting how we met?"

"No," he growled. "But in my defense, the nanny had just quit and I was desperate to get home to Lena."

"At the expense of all the other drivers on the road? That's entitled. I'm not denying that I understand now, but it was also incredibly rude behavior." I stabbed a spicy chicken bite and chewed with a smile while Dante continued to glare at me.

"I can't win with you, can I?"

I shrugged. "There's nothing to win, Dante. You should have been rushing home, but not at the expense of all the other drivers on the road. Your emergency wasn't more important than what anyone else had to do, probably less so because someone you trusted was here, along with probably half a dozen other staff, so really Lena was fine."

His nostrils flared and defiance darkened his gaze. I knew he wanted to argue with me, but he couldn't without coming off as entitled as I'd accused him of being.

"You're a tough cookie, Lucy."

I shrugged. "You have to be when you grow up in the shadow of a beauty queen."

"Mother?"

I nodded. "Decades ago, but she passed the torch on to my sister who is stunning, poised and well spoken, which I decidedly am not. I grew up with everyone comparing me to her, and I always fell short. I grew a tough, thick skin to most criticism." Most people were as callous as they were clueless when it came to so-called well-meaning criticism. "By the time I was seventeen I learned to tune them out.

And by the time I was twenty-three, I learned to love myself all over again."

"That explains it," he said ominously.

Immediately I was on edge, but I took a beat and then another to quell my apprehension before I spoke. "Explains what?"

"Your empathy, and I don't know, the way you talk with Lena is amazing. You encourage her, but in a gentle way that gives her confidence, and then you praise her for what seems like just being herself. It's impressive."

I swallowed around a lump of coal in my throat. "Wow. Thanks, Dante. That means a lot." Most parents considered me nothing more than a glorified babysitter that they paid a premium to, but his recognition of my skills really meant something to me. "You're not just a pretty face."

He laughed, the sound rich and deep, almost soothing. "You think I have a pretty face?"

I rolled my eyes. "I think you know how pretty you are, Mr. Rush."

"Still," he batted his eyelashes and preened. "A guy likes to hear it sometimes."

That brief flash of humor was too much for my poor, neglected hormones to take, especially when I nursed an ill-advised crush on my too grumpy boss.

Chapter 12

Dante

"We're doing fine Mom. I swear. Why would I lie to you?" My weekly video call with my parents was off to an expected start with my mom worried that I was withholding things from her, and my dad backing her up as he always did.

"I don't know Dante, but you have a knack for thinking you have to handle every hardship on your own. You didn't tell us about your divorce until it was a done deal."

I pinched the bridge of my nose and wished I was religious so that I could pray for patience right now. "I didn't want you to do anything that might make Bethany decide to aim for custody of Lena."

Mom scoffed. "As if we would ever."

"Not on purpose, but you definitely would have tried to talk her into making things work by telling her how a little girl needs a mother, which might have resulted in her trying to bleed me dry." Luckily for everyone but Lena, Bethany had no interest in motherhood once she realized that my devotion to my little girl would never transfer to her and her ladder climbing needs.

Mom sighed as if she was offended, but I knew she was merely angling to make me feel guilty. "Well you never gave us a chance to butt in, so I guess we'll never know."

I rolled my eyes. "I grew up with you Mom, remember? I know you better than you realize."

Her cheeks turned a harsh shade of pink that made me and my dad laugh. "Okay well, I concede nothing. Where's my grandbaby?"

"She'll be down soon enough." Lena loved her weekly talks with her grandparents, and any second now she would rush down the stairs excited to recount every second of her week since the last conversation.

"Holy moly, son! When you start dating again you start right at the top, don't cha?" Dad's tone combined with his suggestive eyebrow wiggle drew a frown from me. "She's a real looker. Good for you, son."

I had no idea what the hell my dad was talking about. "Is he all right, Mom?" The familiar sound of feminine laughter drew my attention behind me, and what I saw nearly knocked me off my chair.

Lucy stood behind me in a deep green sundress with pale green flowers, the straps were so damn tiny it was a miracle they kept her breasts contained. She gave a small wave, barely able to contain her laughter.

Mom smacked dad's arm playfully. "For crying out loud, Sam. She can hear you." She turned back to the camera and leaned forward. "He's sorry dear. My Sam can't seem to think straight around pretty young things. Forgets all his decades of training."

Lucy laughed again and shook her head. She was fresh faced with a girl-next-door charm that was only under-scored by her innate sex appeal and the way the dress hugged her curves.

"Lucy," I finally managed to growl in her direction. "What're you doing here?"

"Headed towards the kitchen for something to drink," she said as if it was obvious. "What are *you* doing?"

My nostrils flared. "Talking to my parents," I sighed and turned back to the computer screen. "Lucy Lions, meet my parents, Sam and Cheryl Rush. Mom and Dad, this is Lucy."

She leaned forward, unconsciously giving me a great glimpse at her voluptuous breasts. "Hi Mr. and Mrs. Rush. It's nice to meet you both."

"Dante she *is* beautiful," Mom sighed and held a hand over her chest. "Why didn't you tell us you were seeing someone? Your father and I were getting worried about you!"

Lucy snickered behind me and I chose to ignore her.

"Of course he didn't tell us," my dad grumbled. "This is probably the first time he's been up for air in weeks." Dad cracked up at his own joke, ignoring another smack from Mom.

Lucy joined in and shook her head. "No wonder Dante is such a grouch. Sam you have all the charm in the family."

Dad roared with laughter. "Oh I like her! I like her a lot, Dante."

"You're good for him," Mom said and wagged a finger in my direction.

Lucy sighed. "I highly doubt that Cheryl. Not only is he super duper grumpy," she flashed a smile in my direction, "but Dante is also my boss. I'm Lena's nanny, not his girlfriend," she finally told them.

Mom and Dad both let out disappointed groans and I knew I would pay for that admission later. "You know Lucy, Cheryl and I met on the job. In fact I read that most relationships are formed in the professional arena these days, since all you kids know how to do is work."

Lucy rolled her eyes. "I read that same study," she said with a laugh. "Unfortunately I'm not your son's type, and I don't really go for the grumpy type."

I rolled my eyes while Mom laughed as if she just heard the funniest joke in the world. "He is gloomier than usual these days. Dante when was the last time you had an orgasm? Masturbation may not be ideal, but it will do in a pinch."

Lucy choked on a laugh behind me and I clenched my jaw to avoid glaring at her too. "It definitely does," she added in a soft whisper. "It was nice to meet you Cheryl, and you too Sam. If not for this call I might have thought Dante here was born of cyborgs."

Dad howled with laughter once again. "She's great Dante. Beautiful, got a smart mouth, and funny. If you don't want her I know plenty of eligible bachelors who'd jump at the chance to woo a woman like her."

"You're too sweet, Sam. I think you just made my Christmas card list."

I rolled my eyes and covered them with one hand. This conversation was completely off the rails. "Say goodbye Lucy."

"Goodbye Lucy," she said and laughed when Mom and Dad chimed in too.

"Goodbye Lucy."

She laughed again and waved. "It was very nice to meet you both. Y'all enjoy your weekend."

"You too, sweetheart."

Lucy walked away, but that wasn't the end for me, because my parents spent the next ten minutes telling me that I needed to make a move on my nanny. By the time the call ended, I was half tempted to take their unsolicited advice.

Thankfully, good sense kicked in before she returned, still wearing that too tempting sundress that I was sure would haunt my dreams for the next few nights.

Chapter 13

Lucy

"Where's Daddy?"

I couldn't ignore Lena's worried tone over her father's absence even if I wanted to, because those big blue eyes damn near broke my heart.

I glanced at the clock again. It was after nine and Dante still wasn't home, which was unlike him, and worse, he hadn't called. In fact he hadn't called all day which I'd arrogantly believed was because he finally trusted me to do my job. But now I couldn't deny the fact that something was very likely seriously wrong.

"I'm not sure Lena."

"He always says good night," she whined and her lip quivered.

He didn't just say good night. Dante usually tucked her, read her a story before he kissed her good night and wished her sweet dreams. *Think fast, Lucy.* I had to come up with something before tears or a tantrum came, neither of which were good around bed time.

"I have an idea!" night

"Call Daddy?"

That would be the best idea, but if something had actually happened to him, I didn't want to hear the news with Lena watching and listening. "Better. We'll make a video of you telling him good night and that you love him, so he won't feel bad about missing out tonight. How does that sound?"

"Okay," she said around sniffles.

Relief coursed through me at her easy agreement and I pulled my phone out of my back pocket and set it down before I settled her in bed. "Let's get you under the blankets so he feels like he was right here with you."

"Okay!" She was such a sweet girl, so accepting of everything life had thrown her way, and somehow able to get excited about the smallest things. "How's this Lucy?" She smiled up at me with the blankets tucked up under her armpits.

"Perfect." I held up the phone and tapped the record button. "Okay, what do you want to tell Daddy?"

"Good night Daddy! I love you and I miss you, but don't miss bedtime again, okay? Love you, good night!" She collapsed back onto the bed and sighed. "Was that good?"

"He'll love it," I assured her and sat down on the bed. "I know it's not the same, but I'm happy to read you a bedtime story, if you want?"

"Okay Lucy." Lena settled under her blankets and listened while I read a story about a ladybug who loved to make friends, but she quickly fell asleep. Dante typically made it home for dinner, so since about six this evening Lena had been worried about her father.

"Good night honey." I pressed a kiss to her forehead and sighed as I backed out of the room and turned off the light. I wasn't sure if Lena would sleep peacefully given how the past few hours had gone, so I grabbed my e-reader and curled up on one of the plush sofas in the sitting room.

I was so engrossed in the romance that I didn't hear the front door as it opened and then closed, or the sound of Dante's designer loafers on the floor until his shadow fell over me and my e-reader. His unexpected appearance startled a gasp out of me, but I recovered quickly and looked up with a frown.

"You look like hell." Handsome as hell to be sure, but also like he'd been to hell and back in the ten or so hours he'd been gone.

His scowl darkened. "You don't. What's your point?"

I resisted the urge to smile at his unintended compliment and instead took a long look at his beautiful face. "Rough day?"

Dante nodded and raked a hand through his thick hair as he blew out a long exhale that contained so many emotions that my heart went out to him. "It was a nightmare. Everything that could go wrong today did."

"You want dinner?"

His look only darkened at my question. "That's not your job."

"Duh," I rolled my eyes. "It's called basic human kindness. Look it up when you have a chance." I stood and put some distance between us by warming up the leftover dinner.

"I'm kind," he insisted, his voice closer behind me than I expected.

"If you say so Dante." I turned slowly, which was a mistake, because he was entirely too close, and all of my curves were brushing against him from the front, the counter at my back. "Excuse me."

He took a step closer and I held my breath. "You afraid of me Lucy?"

I laughed. "Hardly. It's just called personal space." I sucked in a breath and skirted around him. "Why don't you go kiss Lena and get changed out of your work clothes?"

He frowned. "Are you a parenting expert now, on top of all your many other skills?"

I rolled my eyes and gave his chest a shove. "You're an ass, Mr. Rush. Lena was worried from the moment you didn't show up for dinner until I managed to get her to go to sleep. She thought something happened to you."

"She knows I would never leave her." He let out an exaggerated scoff just to make sure I knew what he thought about my words.

"Okay fine." I pulled out my phone and sent him the video. "Do what you want, I'm going to bed." I boiled with frustration, so I turned around, ready to grab my e-reader and turn in for the night.

"Lucy," he growled and grabbed my arm to stop me from walking away.

"Let me go, Dante."

"I'm sorry," he growled. "It's been a long day and I'm exhausted."

I shrugged out of his hold and sighed. "All the more reason to go see Lena." I took a step forward and he pulled me back close, but not quite flush against his broad chest. Our gazes collided, his angry and mine shocked. Deep breaths rushed out of us both, and Dante looked as if he wanted to say something, probably scathing to me. In the end, he released me and left the kitchen, stalking up the stairs to his daughter's room.

I let myself have a satisfied smile and rolled my eyes over the stubborn man. He was contrary sometimes just to be contrary, and it was very frustrating, luckily he wasn't my charge. Still, I knew what it was like to have a long hellish day, so I re-heated his dinner before I returned to the living room to retrieve my e-reader once again.

"Stay," Dante ordered as he jogged down the stairs a few minutes later in a fresh pair of lounge pants and a t-shirt that molded perfectly to his chest and arms.

"I am not a dog," I grunted and set my e-reader aside.

He stopped halfway between the bottom of the stairs and the kitchen, his shoulders fell forward and he sighed. "Please stay."

Indecision warred within me. Part of me wanted to

run up the stairs before he returned from the kitchen, just because I could, but that would be petty. Hilarious, but petty.

"Thanks for dinner." Dante returned and dropped down on the sofa, leaving one cushion between us as he kicked his legs up on the coffee table. "It's delicious."

I shrugged and tugged my legs up to my chest. "Don't thank me, Dotty is the one who made it."

"You warmed it up," he insisted with a panty melting smile.

"Job security." I kept my expression blank as a slow smile crossed his face.

"Liar."

I shrugged again and met his smile with one of my own. "You'll never know."

"Thank you for the video. It was sweet and just what I needed." He dug into the food, eating it as if he hadn't enjoyed a meal in weeks. "Even in her sleep, Lena clung to me."

I nodded to acknowledge that I was listening, but I hated that I felt my heart softening towards this stubborn man. Why was it so damn attractive that he loved his kid? He was a father, he was supposed to love and care for his child, and no man should get extra points for doing what mothers have been doing for thousands of years.

"You should call if you're going to be late. I know it's not always convenient, but it would make Lena worry less."

Dante's nostrils flared angrily and I wasn't even

surprised. The man couldn't take any type of criticism. It probably made him a beast of a boss. Then he surprised me by saying nothing, he just returned to his food without a word.

"You know Dante, not every drop of advice is a criticism. It's merely a suggestion, to let Lena be a little girl instead of a ball of anxiety."

His jaw clenched again, but I was undeterred.

"She's already lost her mother, and if you could have seen her worry tonight you would understand my concern."

"Stop!" He barked. "Just...stop Lucy."

My mouth snapped shut and my eyes widened at his tone, or more accurately, my response to his commanding tone. It was hot and forceful, which I apparently liked. "You know, I think I will stop. Good night, Dante." I stood, and this time I didn't take my time, I just grabbed my e-reader and hit the stairs.

"Lucy..." he called after me, but I kept moving, refusing to be derailed by the infernal man. "Dammit."

I couldn't help but smile to myself, that for once in his life Dante wouldn't get his way. Not with me.

"Lucy," he growled again, but this time his hand snaked out and gripped my upper arm.

Where in the hell had he come from? "Didn't anyone ever tell you to keep your hands to yourself, Mr. Rush?"

When he spun me to face him, heat flared in Dante's eyes and I couldn't look away. My heart raced and my breath caught in my throat. "You annoy the hell out of me, woman."

"I feel the same way about you."

He let out a low grunt and then his lips were on mine, his mouth devoured me hungrily, and when his arms wrapped around me to pull me closer, I held on tight. The kiss was hot as fuck, too hot for someone I actively disliked, but damn, he kissed like a dream. His hands slipped from my shoulders down to my waist before he cupped my ass and brought me flush against an impressive length of hardness.

I moaned into his mouth, and his tongue slipped inside. Dante deepened the kiss and stoked the fire that burned through my veins. The kiss was like a revelation, like I hadn't been truly kissed until this moment, which was pretty disconcerting. Still, as much as I told my brain to pull back, to stop this magical nonsense, I couldn't do it. He tasted too good.

Felt too good.

My hands gripped his shoulder and I told myself to use his strength to push away, to end this erotic torture before I did something crazy, like beg him to strip me down and make me scream his name. It was madness and I was powerless to stop it. I leaned into it, devoured his mouth the way he did mine until I was dizzy and horny and out of my mind with lust.

The kiss was eternal, but that was the type of dangerous thinking that I couldn't afford, so finally I managed to slowly pull back, my gaze unfocused and my lips swollen.

"Lucy," he moaned and his fingertips dug into my flesh.

He's your boss. Dammit. I stepped back until his hands fell away, my eyes wide with shock. This was exactly what he expected of me, and all women in fact.

Shit, shit, shit. I took one step back and then another and another until I felt the doorknob of my bedroom pressed against the small of my back. I turned it quickly and stepped in. "I should, ah, get to bed. Early day," I said by way of a totally unbelievable explanation.

"Right," he said shakily. "See you tomorrow."

I nodded absently, slammed the door and pressed my back against it. I kissed my boss. Well, more accurately he kissed me and I did nothing to stop it, which to his warped mind, probably meant that I was trying to find my way into his bed.

Stupid, stupid girl.

I spent most of the night reliving the hottest kiss I'd ever experienced and worrying that Dante would use it as an excuse to get rid of me.

Chapter 14

Dante

I should not have kissed the nanny.

That one thought ran through my mind on an endless loop throughout a sleepless night that finally ended just as the first streaks of dawn painted the sky. It was a mistake to follow her, to stare at those lush lips as she told me I annoyed her as much as she annoyed me. But when I closed my eyes all I could see was the way her eyes fluttered closed a heartbeat before my mouth crashed down on hers.

I knew it was a bad idea to follow her up the stairs after her comments. I should have just let her go to her room and stewed in my anger while I finished my dinner, but I couldn't. And dammit if she didn't taste like fire and sunshine with a hint of whatever chocolate she'd nibbled on after dinner. And as I showered and dressed for the day, there was just one thought running circles in my mind. Now I knew how good she tasted, how her curves felt under my hands and the sounds she made when she was kissed, how in the fuck was I supposed to keep my hands to myself?

The chemistry between us was explosive, I should have known that it would be, because Lucy sparred with me the way no one else did. She gave as good as she got, and had the good sense not to get offended about it too. That was almost as irresistible as her curves.

This was a major problem, because she was the nanny. The hired help. My employee. This had the potential to cause too many problems in my life. Lucy was great with Lena, which meant I had to keep my hands—and my mouth—to myself.

By the time I made it downstairs for breakfast, I felt better about where things stood with me and Lucy. She worked for me, and that was it. Last night was an aberration brought on by a long, exhausting day and a kind gesture, nothing more. There was an undeniable pull between us, and even though she was the first woman who'd fired me up since my divorce, I couldn't go there.

I wouldn't.

"Omelet for you, sir?"

I looked up at Dotty's wary expression and nodded. "Sure an omelet would be great. Egg white omelet, please Dotty." She frowned, and I wondered why. "What?"

"It's nothing, you just don't usually say please." Dotty's lips twitched, but she turned to the fridge before I could ask her more and pulled ingredients from the fridge.

I continued to stare at her back with a frown. Was I

really such a beast that even basic manners surprised the people who worked for me? "I'll try to do better."

Dotty laughed. "It's all right, sir. You just threw me for a loop."

"Morning Daddy!" Lena's voice was loud and cheerful as her feet rushed across the floor to me. "I'm happy to see you!"

I smiled as I scooped her up into my arms and hugged her close. "I'm happy to see you too, sweetheart. Did you sleep well?"

Lena nodded and looked over her shoulder at Lucy, dressed in a loose fitting yellow tank that hugged her breasts, and tight jeans that reminded me of just how good her plump ass felt in my hands. Lucy nodded and Lena turned back to me.

"I did. I had good dreams," she said and wriggled out of my embrace to take her seat at the kitchen table while she told me about rescuing me from my office. "I was a hero."

"Thank you for saving me," I told her as I bit back a smile.

"Love you, Daddy."

My heart squeezed at how easily it came to Lena to be nice and sweet, so full of love. "Love you too, my sweet Lena." My gaze wandered over to Lucy who wasn't glaring at me, but she wasn't smiling at me either, which was a good thing, I told myself.

"What'll it be for breakfast, Lena?" Dotty's voice cut

through my thoughts and I reluctantly pulled my gaze from Lucy.

"Sammich!" Lena danced in her seat and sent Lucy a conspiratorial smile.

Lucy sighed, but her smile was as bright as my daughter's. "Breakfast sandwiches," she clarified. "Bacon and toast with strawberry jam on both sides."

I scoffed. "That sounds terrible."

Then Lucy did glare at me. "Then you don't have to eat it. Stick to your boring egg whites and spinach omelet." She arched a brow in challenge before turning back to Dotty. "It was one of my favorites when I was a kid, and I told Lena we could try it out if she finished her book yesterday."

"I did!" Lena wriggled in her chair again, smiling proudly. "Wanna hear about it Daddy?"

"Of course I do." And I spent the rest of breakfast listening to Lena tell me about a group of baby animals that lived in the jungle and helped each other learn how to survive without their parents. "That sounds like a big girl book."

"Lucy said it was a big girl book."

"Maybe it's too big," I said, my narrowed gaze lasered in on Lucy who stared back defiantly.

"Why?" She folded her arms across her chest, ready for a fight.

It was a good thing I was ready too. "A bunch of orphans all alone in the world? That's too grown up, and probably why she was so scared last night!"

"Or," Lucy said as calm as could be, "maybe she related to the fact that none of them have mothers in their lives, but they still manage to thrive in the world."

"Lucy!" I barked.

"And," she went on in a calm tone, "maybe she was worried because her one remaining parent failed to ease her mind that he *would* be home, just later than usual. But hey, what do I know? I'm just the help, right?" The moment Dotty set two plates on the counter, Lucy placidly cut the two sandwiches into triangles and brought one plate to Lena with a smile. "They just taste better like this. Let me know what you think," she said before she picked up the other plate for herself and exited the kitchen.

"Daddy I think you made Lucy mad."

Yeah well, she made me mad too. "She's fine."

Lena slapped her hands on the table to get my attention. "Don't make her mad Daddy, I like her. What if she goes away?"

Dotty smacked her lips together as she set a cup of juice in front of Lena and refilled my coffee. "Lucy's tougher than that, Lena. She won't let your grouchy old Dad scare her off."

Unfortunately I had a feeling that Dotty was absolutely right. "I'll apologize," I promised Lena to ease the fear that clouded her eyes and furrowed her brow. "Time for me to go."

Lena stood on her chair with her arms extended. "Have a good day Daddy."

"Thank you. Have a good day yourself and I'll see you at dinner."

"Promise?"

I hugged her and smacked a loud kiss to her cheek that made her giggle. "I promise. Love you."

"Love you back," she said, still giggling. "Bye."

I left for the office, my thoughts full of the nanny, to whom I now owed an apology.

I wasn't dreading it as much as I should have been, and that made me consider going back on my word to Lena. Maybe a little bit of anger between us would cool the desire and the chemistry.

Yeah, and maybe pigs would start to fly.

Chapter 15

Lucy

"**A**re you sure it's all right Dotty? I'll clean the kitchen when we're all done, I promise." The last thing I wanted was to increase the housekeeper's workload, but an unexpected rain meant that outdoor activities were off the list for the rest of the afternoon.

Dotty sighed and put a hand on my shoulder. "It's all right, Lucy. I think it'll be good for Lena. She hasn't ever done things like this before."

I frowned. "Ever?"

"No, I'm afraid. The last few nannies were more interested in taking care of Mr. Rush than her."

If Dotty noticed the red blush that crept up my face she didn't say anything, and I was grateful. "Then I absolutely promise to clean up after us. How long until you need to start making dinner?"

"There's two ovens for a reason."

I looked over at the double ovens and nodded. "Alright. We'll work at the table, I think it'll be easier for Lena and that will keep us mostly out of your way."

Dotty's smile was kind and patient. "I can work with that."

"Yay!" I turned and went to Lena's playroom where she was working on a puzzle, her tongue stuck out as she was deep in construction. "Who wants to make cookies?"

Lena looked up with excited blue eyes. "Me! I do! I do!"

"Sounds good. Let's do it." I clapped my hands together and waited while she finished her puzzle and stared at it for a long moment before she turned to me.

"Ready Lucy." She put her hand in mine and we walked back to the kitchen. "What kind of cookies?"

"What do you like? I like peanut butter and chocolate chip cookies, but sometimes I like peanut butter chocolate chip cookies."

She gasped like it was the greatest secret she ever heard. "Yes, please!"

I laughed and guided her to the sink. "First we wash our hands so that we don't end up eating germs with our cookies."

"Yuck," she said and giggled as we washed our hands.

Two hours and dozens of cookies later, I stood back and crossed my arms to stare at our handiwork. Lena took a step back and mimicked my moves as she stared wide-eyed at the cookies. "We did good, didn't we?"

"Yeah, we did." She took a step closer and inhaled deeply. "So good."

I glanced at the timer on my phone as it hit the forty second mark and sighed. "I think it's time for a taste test, what do you say?"

"I say *yes please!*" She jumped up and down, her smile grew wider by the second.

"Peanut butter, chocolate chip or Frankenstein?"

She frowned. "What's Frankenstein?"

I laughed and rolled my eyes because of course Lena is four years old, which meant I had to give her the kiddie version. "It just means that we put different things together to make them one thing. Like a meatloaf sandwich or mac & cheese pizza."

"Frankenstein, please. It's two cookies in one."

"I like the way you think, Lena." I picked up one for myself and nodded for Lena to do the same. She grabbed one and I tapped mine against hers. "Cheers."

"Cheers," she replied loudly and took a big bite of her cookie.

"What is this?" Dante's loud voice boomed in the kitchen over the sound of me and Lena moaning our sugar appreciation. "Are we eating cookies for dinner now?"

"No," I snorted and shook my head. "We're doing quality control, which, as you should know, is an important part of any manufacturing process."

His eyes narrowed to slits and anger radiated off him. "It's just about time for dinner." His tone was hard, and I didn't understand why he was making such a big deal out of one cookie.

"You're seriously worried that one cookie will make Lena not want to eat whatever delicious meal Dotty whipped up?"

His jaw clenched.

"Okay fine, you take the cookie from her and I'll see you in the morning." I shoved the rest of my cookie in my mouth and marched off. Stupid grumpy man who thought schedules were more important than fun and memories.

"Lucy," he called after me.

I kept marching past him and out of the kitchen. "Enjoy your dinner, Lena!"

"I will! Thank you, Lucy, it was fun," she called after me and I couldn't help but smile. The last thing I heard before I closed my door was Lena. "Have a cookie Daddy, they're so good."

Chapter 16

Dante

I took a big, skeptical bite of what Lena had called a Frankenstein cookie, and the minute the peanut butter hit my tongue, my eyes closed and a moan escaped. These cookies were the devil.

"You helped make these?"

Lena's head nodded in an exaggerated up and down motion. "I helped a lot," she said and told me all about measuring out butter and sugar. "I got to roll the cookies and smash 'em too Daddy." She sent me a beaming smile and her eyes glittered with excitement. Clearly she had a fun time today.

Before I came home and ruined it all, apparently. "Great job, sweetheart."

"Can we have another one?"

I laughed at her hopeful expression. "Yes. But after dinner."

Her earlier excitement faded quickly and she nodded. "Okay Daddy. We should ask Lucy to eat dinner with us."

"Lucy knows when dinner is, and if she wanted to join us, she would."

Lena pouted. "Not after you yelled at her. Again." My adorable little girl glared at me like I was the enemy. "Daddy," she whined.

"Okay, okay. If that's what you want, then I'll go up and invite her to dinner." Because apparently we issue formal invitations to employees now.

"I do. Thank you, Daddy."

I resisted the urge to roll my eyes before I turned away and then turned back. "No more cookies until after dinner." I pointed a finger at Lena's smiling face.

"I promise."

"Okay." I inhaled deeply and released it slowly as I climbed the stairs towards the nanny suite. I didn't want to do it, but I promised Lena so I raised my fist and knocked hard on the door. I leaned in close and listened, but there was no noise on the other side of the door so I knocked again.

Again there was no answer.

"Lucy," I growled and knocked a third time, even harder than the first two times.

Nearly a full minute—because I stared at my watch— passed before the door opened and Lucy appeared. "Yes, Mr. Rush, what can I do for you?" She wore a completely innocent expression as if she hadn't heard me knocking. The suite was nice and large, but it wasn't that damn big.

"I wanted to see if you wanted to have dinner with me and with Lena." The words were pushed out through clenched teeth, and though I knew it wouldn't win me any awards, I tried for a smile.

Lucy's eyes widened with alarm and she took a step back. "Was that a smile?"

"Yes."

She tossed her head back and laughed. The sound was deep, lyrical and beautiful, and I wanted it to last forever. "It's good to know you have a few flaws."

I blinked at her words. "I have flaws."

She laughed again. "It's even better than you know that you have flaws."

How in the hell did this turn back to me? "I'm well aware of my shortcomings, thank you. Will you or won't you have dinner with us?"

"I mean, who could possibly turn down such a charming invite?" She shook her head, a smile still on her face. "It's almost as if you don't really want me to attend dinner."

"I asked, didn't I?"

She shrugged. "People ask all kinds of things they don't really want answers for. Like *how's it going*, when you don't really give a damn. Or asking about people's kids when you don't want to know about their latest lost tooth or potty training escapade."

"What the hell is your point?"

"That you don't actually want me at dinner but you're

here asking because you're a good father and you want to make Lena happy."

I blinked in confusion. "You think I'm a good dad?"

Lucy shrugged. "I think you love your kid a lot, and you show up for her, and that's more than half the battle. You could stand to be a bit more present, but parents without your high powered careers have the same problem."

"Is that so?"

She blinked and then patted my chest. "I already said you're a good father, Dante. You want me to write it on a post-it note for you?"

"That would be great, actually."

My words stunned her for several long seconds and then another laugh spilled out of her. "Funny."

My scowl darkened and she laughed even harder. "Is that a yes to dinner?"

Her expression changed, her smile faded and the laughter in her blue eyes turned serious. "I'm sorry, but I'm going to have to decline your dinner invitation tonight."

"Why?"

She arched a brow. "You really need to work on your tone, Mr. Rush."

"I would like an answer."

She rolled her blue eyes as her mouth tugged into a wide grin. "The answer is no, and the why is because I clearly ruined my appetite by eating one whole cooking before dinner."

I stared at her, and her impish smile didn't wither or wilt, instead Lucy stood a little taller, her shoulders squared and her spine straight, ready to take me on if I wanted to fight. "You're a pain in the ass."

She stepped in close, smelling like sugar and vanilla and something I was afraid was uniquely Lucy, and whispered in my ear. "Takes one to know one." Then she erupted in a fit of giggles worthy of any adolescent slumber party.

Her mouth curved up into an exaggerated smile, the corners swung up to sharp points and her toothy smile was fucking gorgeous. My fingers itched to reach out and sift her hair through my fingers, run my palms down her spine, cup her ass and pull her flush up against me again. I wanted my mouth on hers once more too.

Lucy looked up at me and must have read something in my expression, because her laughter stopped abruptly. She pointed at me and took a step back. "Go away. Don't take even one more step forward." Her blue eyes widened almost comically and I couldn't help but laugh.

"You afraid of me, Lucy?"

"Ha! You wish. I'm not afraid, it's called being smart, and one of us has to be."

I took two more steps forward and Lucy took three steps backwards. "Do we?"

She nodded. "Yes. There're all kinds of reasons..." she began and I half-listened as she listed them off, closing the gap between us.

"Lucy?"

She stopped talking and stared at me. "What?"

"Shut up."

She sucked in a breath and her nostrils flared. "Of all the ignorant, pig-headed things...," she began, but she couldn't continue because my mouth was on hers, my hands roamed her body and I smiled to myself because I figured out the perfect way to get Lucy to shut the hell up for a few minutes.

She wasn't exactly quiet, but she wasn't talking, instead she moaned into my kiss and groaned when she pushed her body against mine. Those were sounds I could get behind. Then there was the little whimper she let out when my palm brushed over her hard nipple.

I cupped her ass with both hands and I lifted her in the air easily. Her lush legs wrapped around me automatically, the warmth between her thighs was so fucking perfect I growled at the rightness of it. Lucy's ankles locked behind me and then tightened as her hands fisted in my hair and she deepened the kiss. She was determined to drive me wild, and I couldn't walk away, couldn't end the kiss.

"Dante." She looked at me through lust heavy lids and licked her lips.

I blinked away the fog of desire and frowned. "Shit." I gripped her ass again and lifted her in the air before I set her on her feet. "That shouldn't have happened."

Anger flared in her eyes and she gave my chest a shove, a hard shove. And then another and another. She pushed me until I stood in the hall, still frowning.

"Don't worry, it won't happen again!" She slammed the door in my face which was no less than what I deserved.

I knocked and whispered against the door. "What about dinner?"

Lucy's answer was a loud thud as if she'd tossed something at the door.

"So not coming then?"

A low grunt sounded, followed by another thud.

"More for me," I mumbled to myself and made my way back downstairs to join my daughter for dinner. No sexy nanny distractions involved.

Chapter 17

Lucy

Dammit, that's what I got for being stubborn. My mom would have said that I was cutting off my nose to spite my face, and I would very likely have stuck out my tongue behind her back because she was right. I was a master at making myself suffer just to prove a point, or worse, to make someone else feel guilty for slighting me. It didn't matter if I had to pay for it later, I never regretted it.

Not even now as my stomach growled furiously with hunger, did I regret not taking Dante's dinner invitation. It was well after ten o'clock and I was so hungry that if I didn't get eat something now, I might not be able to sleep properly. I took one last glance at the small fridge in my suite stacked with soda, water and ice cream sandwiches and decided that I was too old to eat ice cream for dinner, which meant I had to venture out of my room and into the kitchen. Sustenance is what my body needed, no, my body craved it at this point, so I snuck down the stairs and hoped like hell that the growling monster in my belly didn't wake up the whole house.

I glanced around the kitchen, checking the oven to see if anything was left warming inside, and then the microwave. Nothing. *Of course Dante hadn't saved me any food.*

"Last time I do him a solid," I grumbled to myself and headed over to the fridge. It was fine that he hadn't thought of me, because a sweet gesture like that might have made it difficult to stay angry and annoyed with him.

Yep, it was aa very good thing, in fact. I smiled as I pulled out everything I would need to make a killer deli style sandwich. Dotty had onion Kaiser rolls in the bread box that were almost the size of my head and I took my time cutting into it and slathering mustard on one side and tapenade on the other, before I stacked it with turkey, salami, pickles, tomatoes and alfalfa sprouts. I took the first bite before I put everything back in the fridge and groaned loud enough that it echoed around the giant kitchen.

"Thought you said you weren't hungry." Dante's deep voice startled me and I choked on a gasp, but then the honeyed sound sent a shiver straight down my spine.

I refused to acknowledge the shiver was from anything more than my skills as a sandwich maker and dove in for another bite. I felt his eyes on me, and since my stupid traitorous body refused to ignore him the way the rest of me was determined to, I turned slowly and stared at him while I chewed. Why did he have to look so damn good? Even now dressed in his expensive flannel pajama pants and nothing else, he made my mouth water even more than the sandwich, which honestly tasted a little worse at the sight of Dante's abs and pecs, and goodness gracious, that trail of dark hair that disappeared behind his waistband.

Stop ogling your boss! I admonished myself and shook the fog of lust away with a shrug. "I felt like a sandwich." I took another bite and that punch of red wine vinegar was so good my eyes rolled back in my head. "Problem?"

Dante's gaze was like a lover's caress as it slid from my face down my neck to the swell of my ample breasts. Too late, I realized that it was the tank top I slept in—without a bra—and my nipples beaded under the heat of his intense gaze.

"No," he grunted. "No problem," he said a little firmer and less grumpy as he turned away from me. "Put some damn clothes on."

Instantly my hackles rose at his tone. "These are pajamas, thank you very much. And if you can't handle it, then maybe you should go away," I growled. "At least *I'm* wearing a shirt," I mumbled under my breath.

Dante turned slowly, and I wish he hadn't, because I was still staring at the broad planes of his back. "This is *my* home."

"Mine too as long as I'm the nanny." I flashed a smile that was guaranteed to piss him off. "Lena's asleep, and I'm hardly dressed inappropriately, so I don't see what the problem is. If you can't stand the sight of a regular woman close your eyes, or better yet, go to your room." I held my smile in place and ignored the sting of humiliation that though he'd kissed me—more than once—Dante did not find me attractive.

Stupid, Lucy.

Instead of another, darker scowl, Dante hit me with a smile and a huff of laughter. "Did you just tell me to go to my room?"

I jutted my chin out defiantly. "I did. I didn't ask you to come down here, you came on your own and then judged me because you don't like what you see. Correct the problem by leaving." I stared at Dante and waited for him to respond, my heart slammed against my chest in anticipation.

His green gaze darkened, heated with desire, and the moment was so hot I swore the kitchen smoldered in anticipation of the fire. Dante's mouth parted ever so slightly and I knew that look, I'd seen it enough times now to know what came next.

I stifled an unintentional gasp and took a step back, one finger aimed right at his shirtless chest. "Nope. Not happening again!" I took a step backwards and then leapt forward, grabbed my sandwich and darted across the kitchen before I paused. Dante stood in the doorway, but there was enough room to slip through if I sucked in my belly and turned sideways, without touching him. That's exactly what I did and when I was free, I darted up the stairs, the sound of Dante's deep laughter trailed behind me.

Chapter 18

Dante

Another week was over, but here I was, allegedly one of Texas's most eligible bachelors, and I was working in my home office late on a Friday night. Lena was in bed after a long dinner of burgers and fries that she and Lucy had made together, which meant I could put in a few extra hours to make up for the fact that I left work at six every day this week to make sure I was home for dinner each night.

One point to Lucy.

I couldn't deny that her unasked for push was just the reminder I needed as to why I worked so hard. Lena's language skills improved by the day, not that she needed any help in that department, and her vocabulary grew as well, which meant she would start school ahead of most of her peers. She'd spent so much time walking me through the steps of seasoning the burgers and making the patties that I had to stop her just to get her to taste some of her hard work. She'd been so proud of herself, and I couldn't stop smiling as she watched my first bite and held her breath until I told her it was perfect.

I opened my phone to look at the photo I'd snapped of her with a wide grin on her face, proud of her, yet sad that my ex had decided that these little milestones were of no interest to her. The next photo was of her and Lucy at the counter laughing together before either of them realized I was watching. Lucy had told a horrible joke, but they both laughed and laughed until they were doubled over.

Lucy was great with Lena, and I was man enough to admit that she was the perfect nanny. Sure she had a smart mouth and tempting curves, but her work with my little girl was transformative. Not that Lena was sullen or behind academically, but under Lucy's particular brand of attention and affection, she was blossoming into a kind, smart and empathetic little girl.

A heavy sigh escaped and my eyes started to droop, which was as sure a sign as any that it was time to call it quits for the day. I turned off the phone screen and rubbed my eyes with the heels of my hands as I stood and stretched my stiff muscles. It was past eleven, but even though my eyes were tired, I wasn't quite ready for bed yet. I headed to the kitchen, for a snack... or maybe a drink, I wasn't sure yet. But I figured I would know it when I saw it.

And I did. Dotty had restocked the giant ice balls for whiskey and I poured a shot for myself just before I noticed the kitchen door that led to the backyard was open and frowned.

"What in the hell?" I was ready to march up the stairs and lay into Lucy for leaving the door open where Lena could wander out and get lost when I spotted the spark of light in the distance. It wasn't enough light to be alarming, just enough to know that it could only be one person.

Lucy herself.

I stepped out and onto the soft cushion of grass. "Lucy?"

My lips curled into a smile at her familiar groan of frustration. "Is lying in the backyard against the rules too?"

"No." I laughed at her impertinence. The other nannies, hell most other women, were so concerned with keeping me happy that they wouldn't dare speak to me that way, but not Lucy. I walked through the grass, and as I approached, I wished I'd kept my distance, stayed back, where it was safe. "What are you doing?"

"Star gazing," she said easily, as if it was a perfectly normal thing to do at nearly eleven o'clock on a Friday evening.

"Why?"

"Why not?" She shot back with a shrug, her gaze never left the dark sky that sparkled with the diamonds of faraway stars. "It's quiet and beautiful out here, and the weather is absolutely perfect."

The weather was perfect, in fact it was overly warm for this time of year, or maybe it was just the sight of Lucy in short denim shorts and a barely there tank top that showed off even more of her ample breasts that the last time we found ourselves in this position.

"This isn't the beach," I growled like the grumpy asshole she accused me of being.

Instead of getting upset, Lucy laughed. Her back arched up and her tits shook as she laughed. At me. "No kidding. I guess that explains why I can't hear the ocean." Her gaze was pure mischief and the corners of her mouth curved up into a smile so bright it rivaled the moonlight. "Have a seat."

I stared at her for a long minute before I dropped down beside her on my back and looked up to the sky. "The stars are beautiful."

"Aren't they, though?" Lucy sighed, a small smile on her lips as she focused her gaze back on the sky. "This is a little slice of perfect."

I couldn't disagree with her words, the sky above was stunning, and the only view more appealing was the one right beside me. "Are you a Texas girl, Lucy?"

She laughed. "Not at all, but I am a southern girl. My family lives in the Atlanta area and my sister was Miss Georgia, so I guess you could say I'm a proper southern girl through and through, though not as proper as my parents would have liked."

"What does that mean?"

"It means I'm polite enough, but not proper. No proper woman of means would end up as a nanny," she laughed, but I heard the bitterness underlying her words. "They told me I was the type to *blend in,* and that I should pick a job that let me do that, but they were thinking wedding or party planner, not a glorified babysitter." She laughed again, but again the sound was harsh and brittle. "I went to school for early childhood development, and this is where I ended up, much to their chagrin."

There was so much to unpack with her words, and I didn't know where to begin. "Are you happy with your choice?"

She stared at the side of my face until our gazes collided. "I am. I make a difference, I have fun and I love my job. What else could I ask for?"

"I don't know, what else?"

"Nothing," she sighed. "Mom was right though, I do best when I blend in."

"Bullshit," I spat at her.

Lucy laughed and there was little joy in it. "It's true. As a nanny for people like you, rich people, I am mostly seen and not heard. I'm a part of the background, rarely noticed or acknowledged, and it's fine. I excel, and then I move on."

I didn't want to think about her moving on with another family or another man. "Your mother wasn't right," I insisted. "There's no fucking way you could ever blend in to anything."

She sighed and turned onto her side to look directly at me. "Careful Dante, you're starting to scare me by being nice or complimenting me, or whatever this is. It's terrifying."

My brows dipped low and I leaned in closer. "I can be nice."

Lucy laughed again as though I'd told a great joke. "Sure."

"I can," I insisted angrily.

She laughed so hard her shoulders shook with it, and as much as I wanted to be upset about it, I couldn't help but smile at her joy even if it was at my expense. I couldn't look away, and more than that, I couldn't help myself as I leaned closer and closer until our lips touched, and fire sparked.

The kiss stalled her laughter, which was a relief, but as my tongue swept across her bottom lip and then her top lip before returning to her bottom lip once again, the fire grew. It spiralled into something hot and exciting and all consuming.

Lucy moaned and arched into me, the stiff peaks of her nipples poked into my chest and my breath caught in my chest, my cock hardened behind my zipper. The kiss grew hotter with every pass of my tongue and I held her closer. Tighter. She moaned again and I pulled her closer.

The feel of her body, lush and soft and pleading was enough to undo all my good intentions and I cupped her ass, pulled her flush against my erection and savored the sounds of her pleasure.

I couldn't get enough and deepened the kiss, holding her as close as I could for as long as she would let me.

Chapter 19

Lucy

Dante kissed me like I imagined he did everything else in his life, with an intense focus and skill that made my head spin. I expected a kiss like the others, hot and too short, yet all consuming. But this time, it was different. Everything was different. His mouth was hot as fuck, his tongue capable and tantalizing, but instead of rushing, he took his time. The kiss was a slow torture that I felt all over my skin, producing goosebumps and a fire that surged through my veins, slow and sensual.

My hands slid down his back to his firm butt and slowly worked their way up his narrow waist, to his broad shoulders, until my fingertips curled in his hair. One leg hitched over his hip until I felt the hot heat of his hard length pressed against my leg.

"Dante," I moaned as his hips ground up against me. How in the hell did I end up on top of him? How had our bodies become so intertwined that I couldn't separate myself from him?

In response to my moaned plea, his hands tightened on my ass, only Dante didn't seem too put out by the extra flesh, the softness of the mounds, as he gripped them and pulled me closer. He tore his mouth from mine with a grunt.

"Lucy, fuck."

I smiled against his mouth and slid my tongue back and forth across his lips from corner to corner, until he gripped me so hard I knew I would be bruised in the morning. My hips ground against his cock and I growled my pleasure, suddenly excited and hungry to see him in the flesh, to feel him surge into me and make me cry out my pleasure.

"Dante..."

He pulled back, his green gaze meeting mine, a question burned in his gaze and I was powerless. I nodded my answer to his unasked question and his lips found my mouth once again, and then my jaw, all the way down to my neck. His lips and tongue kept up a steady torture until he reached the swell of my breasts, licking a trail of heat as his hands snaked up under my shirt. "Yes," I moaned and arched into him as his big hands slid up my back, holding me like I was delicate and petite.

"Oh, nice..." His tongue curled around one hard nipple through my shirt, and in the next moment the shirt was gone and his tongue was on my flesh. "Dante." He growled and continued to love on my breasts, back and forth his tongue circled my nipple and then his teeth sank deep into the soft, sensitive flesh.

Every inch of me was on fire as his mouth worked me over. He sucked one nipple into his mouth and nibbled until I growled before he performed the same action on the other. "Yes," I moaned and arched into him. Letting my hips ground against his erection until he grunted and his hips surged forward.

Immediately Dante switched our positions so he was on top as his hips pressed against me. His hands worked quickly as they slid the hem of my tank top up until the shirt was over my head and flew across the grass. "Fucking beautiful." His mouth took one breast and his fingers tweaked the other until I squirmed at his touch, writhed beneath him while he made me lose control.

"Dante, please."

He chuckled and switched breasts with a growl before his lips and teeth nibbled on my ribcage and down my belly. My right hip. The left hip. He took his sweet time driving me crazy until I writhed beneath him, silently begging him with my body to give me something else, something more.

"Lucy..." he moaned the moment his shoulders touched my thighs. "Fuck." He pulled back and made quick work of my shorts and panties.

I shivered under his intense gaze. I purred, but it quickly turned into a low moan as one finger slipped through my wet slit in a slow back and forth motion that drove me crazy.

"So fucking wet," he grunted and leaned forward to swipe his tongue over my swollen clit. "Hot and wet," he growled and flicked his tongue over my clit again and again.

"Dante," I moaned.

He lifted one thigh over his shoulder and then the other before he inhaled deeply. "So fucking hot and wet. I can feel how much you want this."

"Yeah," I moaned. "What are you going to do about it?"

He laughed. "Just this." He slid a tongue between my slit on one side and then the other, hot and wet against my clit. "And this." He did it again, is tongue curled around my clit before he teased my opening.

"Dante, oh fuck. Yes!" One hand found its way to his head, massaging his scalp with my fingertips. "More," I moaned. "Deeper."

He laughed. "Not yet," he grunted and continued to tease me, first sinking his tongue deep inside of me and then two long thick fingers.

"Yes," I moaned as he filled me perfectly. His fingers plunged deeper and deeper, and I was so turned on I could feel myself sucking those fingers deeper into my core, moaning his name and begging for more. My hips trembled violently and then a spasm jerked through me a second before I clenched around his fingers and tongue. "Dante," I cried out as my body tensed up and my orgasm poured out of me along with a choking sound as the pleasure stole my ability to breathe and talk at the same time.

My hips continued to shudder against his moving tongue, my hips surged forward to prolong my pleasure until my orgasm was completely satisfied. "Mmm, Dante."

His lips curled into a smile and he looked at me like I was something wonderful yet alien to him. "I could do that all night."

"You could," I purred. "But I need something more, a little longer and thicker, if you know what I mean?"

He laughed and got up on his knees before he stood and removed his shirt and loose tie, his undershirt and pants and finally—blessedly—his boxer briefs. "Keep looking at me like that and I won't last long."

"As long as you feel as good as you look, I won't need long."

He growled and stroked his cock, I reached out to help him. "Lucy."

"Dante," I shot back and gripped him in my hands, stroked him long and hard.

He grabbed my wrists and held them over my head, his cock nudged at my opening as his green eyes stared down at me. "You're wet."

"You sure? Maybe you should check again." I arched forward with a moan as the blunt head of his cock slid against me. "Fuck."

His mouth took mine and his tongue slipped inside as his cock slowly sank into me, thick and deep. I tilted my hips and he sank all the way in with a sigh. He pressed into me deeper and deeper, over and over again. He was long and thick and he moved with the kind of slow deliberation that drove me wild. "Dante, yes."

Every word from my mouth moved him differently. Deeper, and then faster, and then his mouth found mine again and worked me over in a hungry frenzy that matched my need for him. My legs wrapped tighter around him and I bucked forward. "Lucy," he grunted.

"More, Dante. Please, I need you."

That was all he needed to hear. One hand palmed my thigh and hitched it up over his hip as he pumped me relentlessly, every stroke hit a part of me that I desperately needed until I whimpered incoherently. "Shit," he moaned.

"God, yes Dante. Fuck me just like that."

He growled again and pounded harder until both of us were slick with desire. "You have a dirty little mouth, don't you Lucy?"

"Something about your cock brings it out in me," I panted and tugged on his hair. "Give it to me," I demanded.

His mouth found mine again and Dante fucked me hard and fast, his tongue thrusting in my mouth in time with his cock. I was lost to the pleasure, the ecstasy of the way he made me feel. "Lucy."

I clenched around him hard and fast, pulsing greedily as he thrust deep. I arched into him as he growled, loud and feral, the sound blended with the wild cry of my orgasm as it tore through my core. I panted, and held on as his hips pumped furiously, finally he stilled, and I could feel him pulsing into me. "Whow."

Dante held me close as his hips jerked with the final throes of pleasure, his lips fluttered on my cheeks, my throat, my mouth. He pumped slowly, until his cock slipped free and then he held me close under the stars like this was more than a quick and dirty fuck, like this was the start of something special.

I relaxed against him until a yawn escaped and sleep threatened. The next thing I knew I was in his arms, floating in the air and then resting on a soft cushion before sleep claimed me finally.

Sweetly.

Gloriously.

Chapter 20

Dante

"Daddy you're smiling!" Lena's sing-song tone yanked me from yet another daydream of last night and the backyard. And the nanny.

"I am. Should I frown?" I asked and twisted my face into a scowl that made my daughter laugh loudly. She was right, I was smiling, and I couldn't stop myself either. I'd gotten an excellent night's sleep, restful and deep. I woke up feeling refreshed and focused. I put in an hour at my home gym and two hours in the office returning emails and going over contracts and designs. It was a godsend to be so well rested since it was Saturday, and that meant it was just Lena and I at home. Lucy and Dotty both had the day off, which was fine with me. "You look very pretty today Lena."

She beamed up at me with a wide smile, her cheeks blushed beautifully. "Thank you, Daddy. You look very pretty too." Lena had picked out a white sundress with yellow polka dots on it and matching yellow sneakers. Her hair was a bit of a mess because I was just shit at doing little girl hairstyles, but she was the cutest thing I'd ever seen. I felt my heart swelling with my undying love for her. She was the sweetest and best thing to come out of my marriage, and I guess I would always be grateful to her mother for that.

I laughed. "Thank you, sweetheart. How are you this morning?"

"Good!" She shouted the words louder than necessary. "What're we doing today?"

I smiled at my daughter's eager face, her eyes lit with curiosity. "It's a surprise," I told her and braced myself for Lena's reaction.

She bounced up and down. "I love surprises, Daddy!" She really did, and no matter what it was, except for trips to the doctor, Lena was on board with it.

"I know you do, and guess what? I love surprising you." Lena was always so grateful, and I hoped that as she grew older, she never lost that sense of wonder and excitement, always up for an adventure.

"What's the surprise?"

I pushed my office chair away from the desk and wriggled my brows as I closed in on Lena, who was so excited she practically vibrated with it. "It's a surprise, that's why it's called a surprise."

"Oh." She smacked both hands over her mouth and her blue eyes widened to saucers. "Right. Sorry Daddy."

"It's okay. There's nothing wrong with being excited. You can ask all you want, but I won't tell you until the time is right."

"Fine," she sighed and reached for my hand. "Are we going now?"

I nodded and kept a smile fixed on my face while Lena chatted nonstop all the way to the park which was twenty minutes away. How a little person with no job and who didn't go to school could find so much to talk about was beyond me, but most of it was—surprise, surprise—about Lucy. The one woman I was trying like hell *not* to think about after last night, but she was all my little girl could talk about.

Last night had been damn near magical. I'd never had sex with anyone outdoors, never mind under the moon and the stars. Lucy was even more sensual than she looked, the way she arched into me and licked her lips, the way she rolled her hips against me when my tongue dipped inside her honey. And fuck me, the sounds she made. I won't forget those any time soon.

"Daddy are you listening?"

I sighed. "Sorry. I was just thinking about your surprise and how much I hope you like it."

"I will," she said with absolute confidence. "The park!" She vibrated in her car seat as we pulled into the parking lot of the city park, so excited she managed to free herself from the harness strap before I could do it. "I love the park Daddy, don't you?"

I scooped her out of the car and set her on her feet.

"Not as much as you do, but yes I do love it here. It's so beautiful." I pressed the button to open the trunk and give Lena her first surprise. "Ready?"

With wide blue eyes she nodded quickly as if a delayed answer might make the surprise disappear completely.

"Okay. This is part one," I told her and set a box on the ground that was nearly as big as she was.

The loudest squeal I heard ever heard escaped from my daughter's mouth when she opened the box. "A princess dress!" The words came out on another squeal and she jumped up and down as she held the dress and screamed, oblivious to the looks she drew from parents and kids alike. "And a tiara!" She gasped and the final piece. "A sparkly wand!"

"I guess you like it?"

"I love it, Daddy! You're the best." She flung herself at my legs and squeezed tight. "My daddy is the best daddy ever!"

"Thanks," I told her with a laugh as I helped her with the dress and tiara. "I'm glad you like it. This will be perfect for the next part of the surprise." I took her hand in one of mine, a blanket and picnic basket in the other as we crossed the park until we came upon the stage.

"A show?"

I nodded and found an empty patch of grass to set us up for the next few hours. Lucy had told me all about the Princess in the Park series, well the truth was she'd left me a flyer with a note on the back that said Lena would love it if I could bring myself to suffer through hours of princess storytelling for the sake of my little girl.

I knew it was a challenge, and though I wouldn't say so to her, I knew Lena and I would end up here because it would make my little girl happy, and because I'd throw it in Lucy's face later. It was a win, really. If the interactive re-telling of *Snow White* was any good, it would be a win all the way around.

I looked around the park at all the exhausted parents who gave half-hearted smiles as they relaxed on blankets and towels, enjoying everything from fresh fruit to sandwiches and even fast food as we all waited for the production to begin. My gaze landed on a familiar curtain of blond hair that hung in loose waves around shoulders I'd kissed every inch of last night.

Lucy.

She hadn't mentioned that she would be attending, but there she was with her redheaded friend, laughing around a yawn that made me smile, knowing I was the reason she was tired. I looked away before Lena followed my gaze, but I'd done it a moment too late.

"Lucy!" Lena spotted her and took off across the park as if she was being chased. "Lucy, you're here! I'm a princess!"

I got to my feet and ambled over to the women, uncertain if I was happy Lena had spotted her or not. I had no plans to chase Lucy, but I couldn't deny that I'd been unable to stop thinking about her all morning. Or maybe my ego was stung that she'd woken up and slipped out of the house before breakfast, at least I thought she had.

"Lena."

She turned to me. "Daddy, it's Lucy. This is her friend Toni."

"I see." My lips curled into a grin at her grown up introduction. "Good afternoon, ladies."

"Fancy meetin' you here," Toni said with an amused grin.

"Lena loves all things princess."

"So I hear," she answered and leaned back, sliding her sunglasses over her eyes. "Have a seat. We have plenty of room and plenty of food."

I looked over my shoulder. "We're already set up over there..." It was a lame response, and if Lucy heard it, she didn't acknowledge it. Or maybe she didn't care.

Toni laughed again. "Too bad you can't move it over here since you nailed it down."

Lena turned from her spot pressed against Lucy's side and gasped loudly. "You did Daddy?"

"No honey, Toni is being a smart as-..., ah she's being a smarty pants."

"Oh." She giggled and turned back to Lucy, both females whispered to each other themselves as they pointed to the stage.

Knowing when I was beat, I went to retrieve our blanket and basket and returned to the women, taking the spot on the other side of Lucy. The moment Lena turned her attention to Toni who'd complimented her tiara, I leaned in close. "Say the word and we'll find another spot elsewhere. This is your day off, after all."

Lucy turned to me, we were so close I could see the depths of the blue of her eyes, much better under the Texas sun than last night under the moon and starlight. "I don't mind. Stay. What's in your basket."

I laughed. "Oh I see, you only want me around for my picnic basket."

She shrugged. "Depends on what's in the basket." She arched a brow and smiled playfully. "I'll show you mine if you show me yours."

It was my turn to arch my brows. "Thought we did that already."

Her cheeks flamed bright red and she looked away before she turned back to me. "We did," she whispered. "And you already know what's in my basket, now I want to see what's in yours."

She licked her lips and my body responded to the unintentionally sexy move. "Touché," I groaned and drew a laugh from the hot nanny.

Lena tapped her arm and Lucy gave my little girl her full attention while she had mine. For the rest of the afternoon I watched Lucy instead of the actors on the stage, instead of the blue skies above. I couldn't look away because she was breathtaking and even though last night was a one off, an event that would never be repeated.

Even though I desperately wanted her again.

Even though I was already thinking of ways to get her alone to take my time, to draw out the pleasure for both of us.

By the end of the play I was certain of just one thing.

I was out of my damn mind.

Chapter 21

Lucy

"You've been keeping secrets little miss sunshine."

Toni's eyes were filled with mischief as she leaned across the table at our favorite diner on the outskirts of town and wiggled her eyebrows.

I sat up a little taller in the booth and lifted my chin high in the air. "What do you mean?" I clenched my jaw tight to avoid laughing at the incredulous look on her face.

Toni pointed at me and laughed. "You know damn well what I mean. Dante Rush couldn't keep his eyes off you throughout the play."

I shook my head. "You're reading into things. He was probably just glancing over to keep an eye on Lena."

She rolled her eyes. "Oh come on, Lucy! You can't be that naïve. The man watched you from beginning to end. He'd totally fail an exam on the play."

I continued to shake my head, not because I didn't

believe Toni, but because I refused to allow myself to respond to what she was saying in any way. "Toni."

"Seriously, just hear me out." Toni picked up her phone and swiped across the screen before she turned it to me. "Look! Just look at that and tell me I'm wrong."

Dammit. I wanted to tell Toni just how mistaken she was, but I couldn't look away from the photo and the look of wanting, of pure desire on Dante's face as he looked my way. He looked like a man besotted with a woman, and before I could pretend I didn't see any of that, the heat of a blush crept up my face.

"Yeah, see." Toni pointed at me again and then at the phone. "That look is *hot!*" Her gaze narrowed and she leaned in closer. "You're hiding something."

"No I'm not." Damn my fair skin that revealed every moment of my embarrassment.

"Yeah," she said a little too loudly. "You are. Spill."

I pulled my lips into my mouth and looked away because I didn't want to admit to what I'd done. It wasn't exactly against the rules of being a nanny, but it was highly frowned upon, not to mention a recipe for unemployment.

"Lucy."

I felt the burn of shame as I turned back to Toni. "Okay. Fine. We slept together." My head fell forward and I closed my eyes, waiting for her judgment.

"You *did?*" There was no judgment in her tone which surprised me.

I risked a peek in her direction, and Toni's expression

was one of shock and excitement. "You're not going to judge me?"

Toni shook her head.

"Or tell anyone?"

"First of all, who would I tell other than you? My reclusive boss who only shows his face once a day? Hardly." She shrugged. "And the only thing I'm judging is that you waited this long to tell me. What's up with that?"

"I don't know," I admitted. "It's not exactly something I'm proud of."

"Why?" She asked with furrowed brows. "Was it terrible?"

"No," I sighed. "It was incredible. So hot under the stars, our skin bathed in moonlight. It was at turns, sensual and raw." I got chills just thinking about it.

"Sounds pretty damn hot to me. So why are you wearing regret like a designer handbag?"

"Because it doesn't matter how amazing the sex was, Toni, I shouldn't have done it. It was stupid and I just know it's going to backfire. How could it not?"

"What, like do you think he's going to fire you for sleeping with him?"

I shook my head. "No, but Dante is, let's just call him mercurial. He's very grumpy most of the time, and I know the first mistake I make, he'll toss it in my face." I had the script of that particular argument half-written in my head already.

Toni's brows knitted into a deep frown. "But you slept with him?"

I nodded and buried my face in my hands. "It's not like I planned it or anything. I was lying out in the backyard gazing at the stars and minding my own business when he joined me. Next thing I know we're naked and that's that."

"Sounds like he was as taken aback by the situation as you were, which means it's not like he can claim you planned it or anything."

"Under normal circumstances I would agree with you, but Serenity made sure to tell me not to dress sexy because all the previous nannies had tried to jump his bones." I knew at some point he was going to accuse me of the same and there was nothing I could do to stop it other than quit now, but I couldn't do that to Lena.

Toni nodded as if she understood. "So he'll say you used your feminine wiles to entice him out to the backyard where you seduced him?"

"Something like that, yeah." I knew I would be holding my breath and waiting for that designer shoe to drop, and in the meantime all I could do was hope for the best.

Toni sighed and fell back against the booth. "It's always the hot ones that are a pain in the ass, isn't it?"

I nodded my agreement. "Is your reclusive daddy the same way?"

Heat flared in Toni's eyes. "That sounds like an erotic romance, *her reclusive daddy*. I think I like it."

I laughed and rolled my eyes. "I wish I had your

outlook on life, Toni." It would certainly give me less reason to worry.

"It's easy, all you have to do is enjoy a healthy dose of not giving a shit each day. It's good for stress and digestion."

"I'll make sure to order some from The 'Zon."

Toni grinned. "They have next day delivery, you know."

"Stop," I laughed. "Thanks for listening, but please let's talk about something else. Anything else."

Toni leaned forward with her chin resting in her hands. "Okay tell me the truth, how big is Dante Rush?"

I rolled my eyes. "Check, please."

Toni laughed so hard it felt as if half the diner turned to stare at us. Toni only laughed harder while my face heated to feverish proportions.

Chapter 22

Dante

I shouldn't be here, and I damn sure shouldn't be doing what I'm about to do.

No matter how many times those words played in my mind on a loop, my feet wouldn't move, wouldn't turn away from the nanny's door and lock myself in my room. I tried. For the past four days I've kept my distance from Lucy by bringing home enough work to get me through to bedtime. I was short and dismissive with her, and I left each morning without breakfast just to give myself some damn breathing room.

Nothing has worked so far.

So here I was, standing right in front of Lucy's door with my fist perched in the air, prepared to knock. Only good sense stopped me, but I knew that wouldn't last for too much longer. I'd gone as long as I could without a taste of her, and now I was craving and desperate for sweetness, and with that thought my fist landed on the door in three sharp knocks. My heart banged around in my chest as I waited, half hoping she was already asleep, or too smart to open up for me, and half wishing I was already inside the room with her.

The door flung open and Lucy stared up at me with sexy, slightly mussed hair, in another one of those damn near see-through tank tops that did wonderful things for her big breasts. The pajama shorts skimmed the tops of her thighs, leaving more leg on display than hidden, and my hands fisted at my sides at the sight of them.

"Dante?" She asked breathlessly.

"What are you doing?" My words came out harsher than I intended, but dammit, why in the hell did she have to be so enticing? So unintentionally appealing?

Her blue eyes widened slightly and she blinked slowly before she hit me with a killer smile. "Reading. What are *you* doing?"

"Losing my mind," I growled and stepped forward into her room until my bare feet sank into the carpet of Lucy's suite. I kicked the door shut behind me without tearing my gaze from her big blue eyes. "I can't stop thinking about you," I growled.

For the first time in our brief acquaintance, Lucy was speechless. My words had stolen whatever smart comeback she'd been poised to make, and I smiled as a sense of deep satisfaction wormed through me, along with a healthy dose of desire. "Um, okay."

"Eloquent," I snorted and took advantage of her sharp intake of breath, her slightly flared nostrils. One hand snaked around her waist and I yanked her flush against me before my mouth crashed down over hers. I kissed her like a man starved for affection, delved deep into her hot mouth as her arms flung around my shoulders and her body molded to mine.

My hands wandered her curves slowly and sensually as Lucy took a step back and then another. I didn't know if she was trying to end the kiss or slow things down and a few seconds later it didn't matter as we crashed onto her bed. I rolled to the side to avoid crushing her smaller frame and brought her with me. Lucy's eyes widened in shock.

"Somebody is happy to see me."

"Always," I growled honestly, not even embarrassed by my admission.

Lucy was so gorgeous as she sat stride me and rolled her hips against my erection. Her head fell back and long blond hair brushed against the tops of my thighs, making me wish I was naked so I could feel the soft swish of her pale blond locks. "Dante," she moaned and her hips moved faster and faster.

"I'm right here, Lucy."

She smiled and licked her lips as her hands moved from my chest to the hem of her tank top, which she quickly removed and revealed pale breasts with dark pink nipples, hard and mouthwatering. Her hands went to her breasts and I growled, moved her hands out of the way and replaced them with my mouth. "Yessss!" she hissed the word out on four long syllables.

I sucked one nipple into my mouth and then the other

while sounds of her moans and cries tore through the air. She moved against me faster and firm, her pleasure rising quickly to the surface. "Ah, fuck Lucy."

She laughed and thrust her fingers in my hair, and held me exactly where she wanted me. "Crazy good mouth," she mumbled before she pushed me back and stood over me on the bed and shucked her tiny pajama shorts and a small cotton thong. "Show me," she purred and hovered over my mouth with a sexy, playful smile.

I sat up and flicked my tongue over her clit until her legs trembled under the force of her ecstasy and she grabbed my hair. "Lucy," I growled.

"Such a good grump." She stepped back and dropped to her knees between my legs, tugging on my pants until they were past my knees and then ankles before she tossed them behind her. "Perfect." She fisted my erection in her hand, giving me hard strokes that made my eyes roll back in my head.

"Fuck!" Her mouth wrapped around the head of my cock and she took me deeper and deeper in her mouth until I hit the back of her throat. "Lucy," I panted and pushed up on my elbows so that I could watch those plump lips rub against my cock. She paused and looked up at me with a smile in her eyes as she took me deep again. It was so fucking hot, and when my hips jerked, she didn't flinch, she swallowed around me. "No more, Lucy. I need to be inside you. Now."

She took her time, sucking me off for another few minutes before she released me with a pop. "Inside me?"

I nodded.

She gripped me in one hand and pushed onto her feet until I was perched so close that I could feel the heat of her body before she took me in and slowly lowered onto my cock. "Ah, yes. So. So. Good." When I was as deep as I could go, Lucy paused and shivered. "Yes."

My hips bucked up and another cry escaped. My fingertips sank into her hips, urging her to move.

Lucy took her time, a sexy smile lit her face as she slowly began to ride me. "Better?"

"Much better," I growled.

She laughed. "I think we can do better," she shot back in a husky tone as she picked up her speed, sliding up and down in long deep strokes that drove me crazy. "Oh!"

I was mesmerized, hypnotized by the jiggle of her gorgeous tits and the way she nibbled on her bottom lip as pleasure quaked her thighs. The small shuddery sighs that escaped her made me impossibly harder, and my fingers dug even deeper into her soft flesh. "Lucy." I gripped her tightly and fucked up into her, the sight of her bouncing breasts and the wide-eyed stare she hit me with brought me even closer to the edge.

She leaned back and rested her hands on my thighs, arching her back as she took me deeper with every stroke. "Yes!" She muttered the word over and over until it had lost all meaning, her body shook violently but she kept moving, desperate for the orgasm that was just out of reach. "Dante," she cried out on a sigh as her body shook and trembled for several long seconds.

I rolled us over so that I was on top and gripped the inside of her thighs in my hands as I pounded in hard, fast strokes that hit her perfect spot with every pass of my hips. "Ah, Lucy. Babe." I rested my head on her chest and thrust hard and deep, again and again until another orgasm erupted out of her on a low wail.

"Fuck, Dante. Yes! Yes!" Her hips bucked wildly and she pulsed around me so tightly, that in mere seconds my own orgasm ripped through me.

Her name escaped on a roar and I collapsed on top of her soft form. "Sorry," I muttered against her shoulder.

"Don't be," she sighed. "You feel nice. And that was really hot."

I laughed. "So fucking hot." Eventually I regained feeling in my muscles and rolled to the side with a long sigh. I watched Lucy as she turned to face me, a sleepy smile on her face. "Was that okay? I mean, not too rough or anything?"

She rolled her eyes. "Did you miss the *really hot* part?"

"No," I laughed and shook my head because she deserved an explanation. "I tried to stay away from you. For days you've been on my mind, my every fucking waking thought, and I made myself stay away."

"I noticed," she said softly.

"I had to," I said almost frantic. "I figured that coming here and seeing you would remind me of why we shouldn't be doing this." It was a shitty thing to say considering our bodies were still coated with each other, but it was the truth.

Her smile dimmed, but she nodded as if she understood. "Did it remind you?"

"No," I growled.

Lucy laughed and pushed away from me. "Sorry to disappoint you."

I sighed and rested a hand on her thigh. "The last thing I am is disappointed, Lucy. Watching you ride my cock was so incredibly sexy, I don't know how I'll stay away now."

She sighed and turned away, giving me her back. "It's not like I was looking for this either, Dante. Whatever else you might think of me." Her tone was almost defeated and I frowned.

"What did I say?"

"Nothing," she answered and shrugged off my touch. She stood and faced me. "I know I'm not what you want Dante, not for real. But I don't need to hear it when your sweat is still dripping off my skin."

I sighed and reached out to her, pulling her back until she was half on top of me. "That's not what I meant, Lucy. I want you, more than I should considering that you're here for Lena. I don't like feeling out of control and being unable to stay away from you is a form of losing control."

"And the world will end if you lose control?"

"No." I huffed out a laugh. "It won't end, but I was so angry during my divorce, and the fact that my ex refused to even fight for Lena..., well, I lost my shit more than a few times." I hated to even think about that time in my life. "If not for the fact that she didn't want Lena, I might have lost my child, I'd gotten so crazy and out of control."

Her blue eyes widened and I waited for the fear or the judgment, but her lips curled into a small, sympathetic smile. "I can't picture you losing control like that. You're so self-contained, but maybe that's why you're so gloomy. Holding everything in like that would piss me off too."

I squeezed her tightly and she squealed. "I'm not *that* grumpy."

"You are, and if you weren't so hot people would totally hold it against you."

"You mean if I wasn't so rich," I corrected her, because that's what most people saw first.

Lucy snorted. "Rich people just have a lot of money, and that's pretty easy to hate no matter what. But you're so stupidly good looking that I'm sure you get away with a lot more than you should."

I frowned at her words. "You're telling me my face is more appealing than my wealth?"

She shrugged. "It wasn't your wealth that stopped me in my tracks on the road that day. It was the tall, dark and handsome part of the equation. Otherwise, you would have been just another rich jerk."

I couldn't help but laugh at her assessment. "That's definitely a first for me."

She turned to me earnestly, her expression had changed from playful to serious. "You're a grumpy ass most of the time Dante."

"Thanks?"

She giggled. "It's the truth, but you're very sweet with your daughter, and despite your grouchy attitude, you make sure Dotty doesn't work too hard and you ask your employees about their private lives. You're not a *total* ass, but this is...new to me. I don't, ah, I don't get this close to the men I work with, or for. Not ever."

I'd heard that before, too many times to count. "Never?"

"No, never. I can't deny there's something about you even beyond that pretty face, a chemistry that surprised me. But if you don't want this, then neither do I. You can go back to your room right now and this will be it. No harm, no foul."

Her words surprised me. She was the first woman, other than my ex-wife, who had willingly walked away from me, and Bethany had still taken a few million dollars for her troubles. Was this offer too good to be true?

I must have waited too long to respond, because Lucy slowly pulled out of my hold and slid away until she was all the way on the other side of the bed. "I get it, Dante. We'll just pretend that this night, and the other night, never happened. It'll make things easier," she said softly. "For both of us."

"Lucy," I called after her as she started towards her private bathroom.

She turned just inside the bathroom and tried for a smile that didn't reach her blue eyes. "I like working with Lena, and I'm a professional Dante, I promise things will go back to normal."

134

I frowned and sat up, unhappy with every single fucking word she just said to me. "What if I can't let this go?"

She sighed. "Then I guess you'll replace me and we'll both move on with our lives." She gave me one long look that felt suspiciously like goodbye before she slipped inside the bathroom and closed the door.

I don't know how long I sat there on her bed and listened to her in the shower, wondering if I should join her or leave her the hell alone. I knew I couldn't leave her alone, not yet. I hadn't had enough of her and I wasn't ready to walk away from her yet, but she worked for me.

I got to my feet slowly and stared at the two doors, one led out of this room and back to life as usual, and the other led to Lucy and her lush curves and easy smile.

Left or right.

Normal life, or Lucy in full vibrant colors.

The choice was easy.

I turned left and slipped inside the bathroom and into the shower, spending the rest of the evening losing myself in Lucy, in her laugh and her sweetness.

Chapter 23

Lucy

"I t's still raining," Lena whined for the third time in less than thirty minutes.

I felt her pain. Nonstop rain forced us to stay indoors and limited the fun activities we could do. "I know it's no fun to stay inside all day, but I was thinking of something interesting we could do." I waited until I had the little girl's full attention. "We can learn Spanish." I tried to inject as much of an upbeat attitude as I could to make sure she was excited about it too. *"Hola, mi nombre es Lucy."*

Lena's eyes grew as wide as saucers. "Hola," she began and spoke a bunch of gibberish before she ended with, "Lena."

I kept my laugh lighthearted, but her eager attempt was a good start. "That means hello, my name is. Ready? I'll go slow this time."

She nodded and rushed to my side with an adorable smile on her face. "I'm ready!"

We spent nearly an hour learning basic Spanish words and phrases, things Lena would use often and would be unlikely to forget. I figured it was Texas so learning a bit of Spanish would be helpful, and small kids loved to learn new languages. But as we passed the hour mark, Lena's focus began to drift and I knew it was time to do something else, anything that wouldn't remind me of the time I spent with her father. Naked. Sweating and panting. In the shower.

"Lucy, doorbell!" Lena gripped my forearm as if she'd been trying to get my attention for some time.

I looked around and didn't see Dotty anywhere, so I assumed she was busy in some other part of the house. "Hold your horses," I muttered under my breath as the bell rang again, and then again, even more insistently. I yanked open the door and froze, not just because the man with the dimpled smile was gorgeous, but he was also familiar. Very familiar.

"Alex Witter."

His smile widened. "Very good. And you are?"

I blinked and gave myself a moment for the shock to fade. The running back for the Houston Highlanders stood just a few feet from me and I felt like a fan girl. *Say something, dummy.* "I'm Lucy, the nanny. I assume you're looking for Dante?"

Alex nodded, a slightly amused expression on his face. "I am."

I took a step back and motioned him inside. "He's at work." Alex Witter was here, and my first thought was that Toni would love to meet him. My second thought was less friendly. "You're *that* Alex." The one who was on the phone making fun of me with Dante.

"Hey," he held his hands up in a defensive gesture. "I didn't say anything. All I did was ask if you were hot." His gaze raked up and down my body, and despite how drop dead gorgeous he was, I felt nothing.

Soon enough the sound of tiny sneakers on the floor grew closer and Lena squealed with excitement. "Uncle Alex!" She kept running and leapt at Alex who caught her easily—because *of course* he did—and scooped her up in his arms. "Holy smokes Lena, you're a big girl now. No more diapers?"

She giggled. "No more diapers. I'm a big girl. *Hola*, Uncle Alex."

"*Hola Lena. Cómo estás?*"

She looked to me with a confused stare and I smiled. "You say, *Soy buena*, I'm good."

Lucy turned back to Alex with a wide smile. "*Soy buena*, Uncle Alex."

"Very good," he chuckled and pressed a loud kiss to her cheek.

"Daddy's not here."

"So I gathered," Alex answered with a smile and carried Lena to the sitting room, obviously he was familiar with the place.

I followed behind and let it settle in that I'd slept with someone who knew Alex Witter personally. Oh wait, I'm pretending we didn't sleep together, so no, I just work for someone who knows someone famous. Nothing more.

Dotty entered the living room just as we did and Alex perked up. "Dotty! How are you beautiful?"

The friendly housekeeper smiled, and if I wasn't mistaken, a blush turned her cheeks pink. "Alex Witter. I hope you're using those hands to catch balls and not more drama."

"Aw, Dotty you wound me." The smile on his lips said he enjoyed her semi-affectionate words. "I don't catch drama, it just follows me. That's part of why I'm here, a break from the spotlight."

Dotty nodded. "I'm just finishing up lunch, so I hope you brought your appetite."

"I take it with me everywhere I go, especially here."

Dotty's cheeks turned a deeper red and she rolled her eyes before returning to the kitchen.

Alex sat down and took up far too much real estate on the sofa with his big frame. He knew what he was doing, and when I saw the challenge in his eyes I kept my distance. "So, Lucy..."

"So. Mr. Witter."

He laughed. "That's my pops. I'm just Alex."

"So. Just Alex."

He laughed again. "I like you, Lucy."

"I like you too," I told him. "Except when you're

playing the Tornadoes, you can't seem to get away from their fullback."

Shock was written all over his face. "Beautiful *and* she knows football. Tell me you're single."

I rolled my eyes. "Not your type, remember?"

"Those were Dante's words, not mine. But now that I've seen you up close, I know why he said that."

Ouch. Hurt and anger coursed through my veins at his words. Maybe he was as big a jerk as Dante. "Cool. Good to know," I said as calmly as I could manage. "Come on Lena, let's get washed up for lunch."

Alex was the best running back in the country, so I knew there was no way to outrun him, but that didn't mean I had to speak to him. "Hey Lucy, you've got it all wrong."

I shrugged. "It's fine, Alex. No harm done."

"Bullshit."

"You said a bad word, Uncle Alex."

"Sorry honey, I mean to say bull poop." He smiled and made Lena giggle before she ran off to the kitchen. Alex turned his attention back to me. "What I meant was that Dante only said that to keep me away from you. I mean seriously, what man doesn't love a curvy blond with a smart mouth and more than a working knowledge of football? If I wasn't so sure he wanted you for himself, I'd whisk you away to Hawaii for the weekend." He wiggled his eyebrows.

"Put that charm away, Alex." Because unfortunately

there was no spark, dammit. Why, oh why did it have to be Dante who revved my engine?

"Fine. So how's this new gig coming along?" He asked as we both made our way to the kitchen.

"Great. Lena is a sweet little girl and she's very smart."

"A very diplomatic answer." He smiled wide and dug into Dotty's delicious three-bean chili with all the fixings.

"Thank you. I try." I topped my chili with sharp cheddar and jalapenos while Lena requested I add a mountain of cheese to her bowl. "Are you really here to escape trouble?"

Alex shrugged. "More like to escape the temptation of trouble, but also to see how the new nanny was working out."

I smiled because I knew what he was doing, and if Dante hadn't confirmed his feelings I might have been tempted to believe he'd said something to Alex about us. "You're a good uncle to be so concerned about Lena."

He laughed to himself. "It's her workaholic father I'm worried about."

I shrugged and took my time chewing. "Luckily for me, it's not my job to look after grumpy men." Dante was more than capable of dealing with—or avoiding—his own emotions. "But Lena and I get along great, so don't worry your pretty little head about her."

Alex stared at me for a long time before he let out a bark of laughter so loud it startled Lena. "You're feisty."

"I've been told that on occasion."

He continued to laugh. "I'm sure Dante hates it."

"You would be correct," I confirmed with the barest hint of a smile.

"Oh man, I wish I could move in just to see it all unfold." Alex shook his head and I could see that he and Dante had a genuine friendship. And if I was looking to torture myself, I might wonder if Dante was different with Alex than he was with me or the rest of the world. But that was absolute madness and I refused to go down that path.

"Nothing to unfold. I update him on Lena's days and her progress, sometimes I eat with them and that's it."

"Bullshit." He froze and slid a gaze to Lena. "Sorry, sweetheart."

"Bullshit," she shot back with a smile.

"Your fault," I told him and pointed an accusatory finger in his direction, but I couldn't help chuckling.

Lena started to laugh and finally Alex joined in and the more we all laughed, the more we continued to laugh. It was a good, cleansing laugh, the kind that made the sides ache.

"Am I paying you to line up your next date, or to look after my daughter?" Dante's harsh words cut through our laughter like one of those sharp Japanese knives.

His words were sharp and painful just as he meant them to be. I turned slowly and met his angry glare, so full of hate I visibly winced. "Dante," I began and corrected myself. "Mr. Rush, your friend stopped by unexpectedly."

His lips curled into a sneer, his green eyes so dark they were black. He huffed out a bitter, angry laugh. "Decided to trade up, I see? Sorry to disappoint you sweetheart,

Alex might be more famous, but I'm richer. Looks like you made a bad trade."

His words pissed me off and I gripped the table so hard that my fingers started to ache. Tears swam in my eyes, but I refused to let them fall in front of him. I refused to give Dante the satisfaction of knowing that his words had impacted me in any meaningful way. I swallowed my emotions and stood slowly, my anger bubbled up as I pulled myself to my full height. I turned to Lena who wore a wide-eyed expression full of fear, and then to Alex who looked both sympathetic and angry.

I wanted to say something to both of them, to ease their minds, but I couldn't speak. I knew if I tried I might burst into tears, and that wasn't going to happen. No way in hell. I took a sip of water and inhaled a deep, fortifying breath before I made my way to Dante. "Am I dismissed for the evening?"

His nostrils flared, but a hateful smile tipped up the corners of his mouth. "You're dismissed." He spat the words at me just in case there was any doubt as to how he felt about me.

I gave a short nod, stepped around Dante and rushed up the stairs two at a time, slamming the door behind me so loud it echoed in the hallway outside. Only when I was alone in my suite did I let my tears fall. It was silly to cry over a man like Dante. He wasn't mine, and he would never be mine, whether I wanted it or not. It didn't matter that I had started to like him, to be able to see past his grumpiness to see that he was a good father, a kind man and good to his employees.

He's also a total asshole, I reminded myself to stop me from extolling his virtues. I didn't care that he was good to the people in his life, it was literally the bare minimum of what a decent human being should do.

Dante Rush was a jerk, and I needed to remember that the next time I started to forget.

Chapter 24

Dante

I stood rooted to the spot when I heard the sound of male laughter as I entered my home. Jealousy mixed with white hot rage roared through me at the sight of Lucy laughing with Alex, and I didn't like that feeling at all. It wasn't me. I didn't *do* jealousy, and I certainly wasn't about to get all googly-eyed over the nanny, even if I could still smell her on my skin days later. Even if I couldn't get the sound of her erotic moans out of my head.

But there she was, laughing and flirting with the best running back in the country as if she hadn't had my cock in her mouth days before. It pissed me off and I reacted badly. Her fake tears wouldn't work on me, even if she did that magic trick where they never fell, just stayed there as some sort of guilt trip.

"That was mean Daddy," Lena said with a disapproving frown. "What's a date? And how much money do you have Daddy? Must be lots!"

Alex choked on a laugh and put a hand on my daughter's back. "He has lots and lots of money, love. You should probably give me back the Swear Words money." He held out a hand and Lena stood on the kitchen chair and slapped a few bills into Alex's large hand.

"But you said *bullshit*," she whispered.

He laughed again. "Good point, alright, you keep this then."

With a satisfied smile, Lena tucked the money back into her pocket and returned to her food. "Okay."

"Is that chili I smell?"

"It is," Dotty responded, her tone short and crisp. "It's on the stove, I'm sure you can find your way there," she grumbled and left the kitchen.

I frowned at Dotty's back wondering what in the hell had gotten into her, but shrugged it off and set my work bag down before I moved further into the kitchen and washed my hands a little harder than I needed to.

"Can I go color Daddy?"

"Yeah, sure honey."

Lena darted out of the kitchen without a care in the world and I envied her in that moment. The kitchen was silent, oppressively so, as I piled a bowl high with chili. "Just say what you have to say," I barked at Alex.

He sighed loudly enough that I could almost feel his irritation with me, but I didn't care because I was irritated with him too. "You were too harsh with Lucy."

"What are you, standing up for your girlfriend now?"

He snorted a laugh. "You sound like a childish asshole,

146

you know that right?" He shrugged. "And worse, you sound jealous. I wonder why that is. All of this in front of Lena too."

I took the seat across from my best friend and glared at him. "Her job is to watch my daughter, not flirt with any man that rings the door bell."

Alex stared at me with a serious expression before a loud laugh exploded out of him. "Flirting? You're not serious, are you?"

I nodded and shoveled another spoon of chili in my mouth.

"You're ridiculous, not to mention so jealous you can't see straight."

"I'm not jealous," I growled. "I know what I saw."

Alex rolled his eyes and sat back in his chair, folded his arms and glared at me. Hard. "I know when a woman is flirting with me, and let me tell you that Lucy wasn't. She was nice to me, that's all."

That was bullshit. "You mean to tell me that you showed up and she didn't respond?"

He smiled. "She was shocked to see me on your doorstep, yeah, but that's probably because you didn't brag that your best friend is Alex Witter. Then again, why would you when you're *so much* richer than me?"

Okay, I felt like an asshole for that. "Sorry. I was just upset."

He shrugged. "It's okay, man. I'd be upset too if I thought someone was trying to steal her from me." His gaze narrowed angrily. "For the record, I would *never* try to steal your girl, and the moment I saw her, I knew exactly why you said she wasn't my type. You wanted her for yourself."

I opened my mouth to deny it, but Alex shook his head.

"You think I don't know when a woman is interested in me, or more so, in the superstar version of me? Trust me, I know exactly who likes me for me and who doesn't, and Lucy wasn't giving off any kind of bad vibes. Called me out on my record against the Tornadoes, if you can believe it."

I smiled. "She doesn't give anyone an inch." And why didn't I know she was a football fan?

"If anything, she treated me like I was her boyfriend's best friend, not a potential date." Alex let his words sink in and then he laughed, at me. "You screwed that all to hell though, without any help from me I might add."

"I'm not a child Alex and I don't need you to spare my feelings."

"Believe me," he laughed. "I'm not. You were an ass to her and you don't deserve to have your feelings spared, I'm just telling you that she didn't do what you crassly accused her of doing. She's a nice woman, and a fan, nothing else."

Shit.

"She's going to quit." And not only will I not get to see Lucy every day, but I'll have to start the nanny search all over again. The thought of that didn't sit well with me. As much as I pretended to dislike having her around, I liked having her here. I looked forward to it, dammit.

"Way to worry about the important things," Alex snorted. "She likes the job and has nothing but good things to say about Lena, so she probably won't quit. But whatever was happening with you two is probably over."

"Who said anything was going on between us?"

Alex rolled his eyes. "Seriously? I've never seen you get that bent out of shape about a woman you haven't slept with." He shrugged. "Besides, I got to know her a bit, and I would've been just as pissed off as you are right now if I thought I was about to lose her."

What he didn't say, didn't have to say, was that my behavior had made me lose her anyway. "What're you doing here anyway?" I asked, changing the subject from my fuck up to Alex's. I knew the man well enough to know that if he managed to drag himself away from his glamorous lifestyle to my relatively boring home, he'd done *something*.

"I was in the neighborhood," he said, deflecting. I decided to let him off the hook for now and not press the issue. He'd tell me when he was up to getting whatever was weighing him down off his chest.

"I need to check on Lena." It was a lame excuse, but I needed a moment to myself. Alex was a lot of things, but he wasn't a liar, had never lied to me anyway, and he wouldn't have hesitated to give me shit if Lucy had flirted with him. All of that meant I had horribly misread the situation and said terrible things to Lucy.

I need to apologize.

But somehow I felt myself hesitating as I left the

kitchen. Probably because I couldn't think of what I could possibly say that would redeem myself to Lucy. Later. I would apologize later.

After I checked in on Lena, finding her busily coloring in her unicorn colouring book, I went out back and found Alex out on the terrace with a beer in his hand, his gaze unfocused on the distance. "Are you sure you're all right?"

"I'm great," he answered in that breezy way of his. "Just needed a break and figured I'd come see you. Maybe you should stop worrying about me and go apologize to Lucy."

"I will, once she's had time to cool down."

Alex shrugged. "If you wait you're just giving her time to come to terms with leaving Lena. And you."

I sighed heavily and shook my head. "Right now, we both might say something we regret, which will result in the same thing, her leaving. I need to clear my head first."

That moment never came though. Lucy refused to join us for dinner, and when I stood outside her door before heading to bed, there was nothing but silence.

There would be no more midnight sandwiches, unfortunately.

Chapter 25

Lucy

I can't even be surprised because I knew this would happen.

I knew Dante would turn into an even bigger jerk than his default setting, which should have been reason number one to avoid getting tangled up with him, but I didn't think it would happen so soon. I figured, in my eternal optimism, that it would take a few weeks of naked time before he reverted into acting like an ass instead of ending things.

But things played out the way they had, and no amount of wishing or overanalyzing was going to change that, even if that's what I wanted.

Thankfully it wasn't what I wanted. I didn't want to change a thing that had happened, because I was a firm believer in believing people when they showed you who they were. Dante thought that I would *trade up* as he called it, and not just with some rich guy, but with his best friend. That's what he thought of me.

So I kept an emotional distance the way all childcare professionals were advised to do. It was difficult to be emotionally detached when dealing with small, vulnerable children. It was easy to let yourself pretend you were part of the family when you were nothing but the help. An employee. It was a lesson I'd learned the hard way when I first started out, and even though I promised myself I would never make that mistake again, here I was.

Making that same mistake, no not the same mistake, but worse this time round.

So yeah, I kept an emotional distance for the rest of Alex's visit and beyond. I made sure I never forgot my role again. I was the nanny. Paid to teach and babysit Lena, nothing else. I wasn't a family friend or a girlfriend or a lover. I was paid to be here and allowed to live in a suite of rooms as part of my salary. So I stayed in my room when I wasn't on the clock. No more family dinners or movies. It was a lonely existence, but it gave me plenty of time to research fun but educational activities to do with Lena.

Thursday evening rolled around, and I sent a quick message to Toni, hoping I wasn't interrupting her with her charge. "Is it all right if I stay at your place this weekend?"

She replied immediately. "You don't even have to ask."

I smiled, grateful to have such a good friend. "I just wanted to check since you refuse to let me pay rent." I knew she didn't need the money, but it made it hard to think of the spare room as mine when I didn't pay for it.

My phone rang instantly and I answered with a smile. "The place is paid for Lucy, and I'm not in the habit of making money off of my friends. If you want to help out, keep it clean and pick up the mail, and feel free to stock the fridge with snacks and booze."

I sighed. "I can do that. Thanks Toni."

"No worries. Do you want to tell me what happened?"

"Not particularly." I didn't want to talk about it at all. It was humiliating, and I'd rather just forget it. But Toni was my friend and she deserved some sort of answer, so I gave her a quick rundown that started with the kitchen kiss and ended with him basically calling me a slut. "The other shoe has dropped."

"That son of a bitch!" Toni was furious and called Dante every name in the book. "Want me to kick his ass for you? Because I totally will."

"No," I sighed. "It's not all that serious. It happened, and it's over and in the past. I'm over it, or I will be soon enough." That's what I told myself every morning, and soon enough, it would be the truth.

"So you're not leaving?"

"Hell no, I'm not. I'm here for Lena and I'm not going anywhere. This is also one of the best paying gigs I've gotten in a while, I have to think of my financial future." I did have to seriously think about it, because at the end of the day, I had no one but myself to really rely on. I had to be able to take care of myself. Dante might be a complete asshole, but he paid well.

"Are you sure?" Toni's concern almost made me doubt myself.

Almost. I nodded even though she couldn't see me. "Yes, I'm sure. In time I'll forget it, and one day it'll be like a fuzzy memory of something you know happened, but can't quite make out the details." At least that's what I was telling myself. "I have to believe that."

"Well," Toni sighed. "It sounds to me like you're falling for him and your heart is breaking a little each time you try to convince yourself that you can forget him and just maintain a professional relationship."

"I'm not," I insisted, but even as I uttered the words, my heart ached at the denial and I wondered if I really was just lying to myself. "I wouldn't do something that foolish." Sleeping with Dante was foolish enough.

"It's not like it's something you can help, you know. You're just human."

"Doesn't matter. Nothing is going to come of it. I'll see you this weekend Toni, thanks again."

One more day, I told myself as I ended the call with a sigh. The weekend couldn't come soon enough. I would have peace and quiet, space to walk around the apartment, and best of all, a home-cooked meal. Until then, I opened the small fridge and pulled out a salad and a can of strawberry pop. It was nowhere near as good as Dotty's salads, but it was enough.

And that was the sad story of my life.

Growing up, my parents were always too focused on my sister's pageant career, and I told myself at the time that the love that was left for me was enough. Same thing with boyfriends, the little time they could give me was enough, their mild affection wasn't love, but it was enough.

I've had enough with enough!

But tonight, grocery store salad was all I had, and it just had to be enough.

Chapter 26

Dante

"I'll be back on Monday Lena, I promise." Lucy crouched down in front of my daughter with a sad smile on her face and she held her pinky up. "See? I promise."

Lena sighed heavily and flung herself at Lucy, wrapping her little arms right around her, she squeezed tight. "Promise?"

Lucy smiled and nodded as she hugged Lena tightly. "Yeah, I promise. I'll see you on Monday, and I have a surprise for you. Have a good weekend." Lucy stood and picked up her overnight bag with one hand and ruffled Lena's hair with the other. She pulled open the door and walked through it without a glance back at me.

I couldn't deny how much that stung even if I deserved it. "All right Lena, come on."

"I wanna go with Lucy, Daddy."

"I know sweetheart, but Lucy can't work every day of the week, can she?"

"No." She shook her head and sniffled. "That's not fair."

"Exactly." I scooped her up in my arms with a smile. "But like she said, she'll be back on Monday. For the next few days, it's just me and you kiddo."

Lena grinned and nodded. "What are we gonna do Daddy?"

That was the question, wasn't it? I'd relied so heavily—okay, *too* heavily—on Lucy to plan outings and events over the past few weeks that I didn't even know where to begin. "We'll find something, I just know it. How about we go out for dinner tonight, just you and me?"

Lena bounced excitedly and pushed out of my arms before she raced up the stairs to pick out something to wear. I couldn't help but smile at her excitement. At least my little girl still wanted to spend time with me.

I went in search of Dotty to let her know she could knock off early and found her in the laundry room. "Hey Dotty, I'm taking Lena out to eat, so you don't have to worry about dinner."

She shrugged but didn't turn to look at me. "I'll just pop it in the fridge and you can have it tomorrow. Or not."

I frowned at her surly tone. "Have I done something to offend you?"

Dotty shoved the last of the towels into the washing machine and glared up at me. "Offended? No. I'm disappointed in the way you spoke to Lucy. She's a nice girl with a good heart, and you," she pointed at me angrily. "You and your angry words broke her spirit. The girl hasn't had a proper dinner all week because she refuses to leave her room."

"That's not my fault," I insisted even though we both knew it was.

"Sure," Dotty groaned as she yanked sheets from the dryer. "Must be someone else who impugned her character in front of Lena as well as a virtual stranger." Dotty glared at me, her anger palpable and her tone accusatory.

The woman who'd been so reliable, my trusted employee for so many years, was now furious with me. "Dotty, I'll fix it. I promise."

"If you can," she grumbled and pushed passed me with the laundry basket in her hands. "If not, just know that I won't be doing double duty as babysitter and housekeeper." With those words, she was gone and I was left staring after her, shocked and slightly amused despite the situation I now found myself in. A situation of my own making.

Everyone, it seemed, was on Lucy's side, which only made me feel worse, like an even bigger fucking jerk because there had been witnesses. Alex and Dotty had witnessed my bad behavior, which meant that I couldn't forget it if I wanted to. All that was left was to apologize. To make it right.

I made my way upstairs to change into something

appropriate for the somewhat fancy dinner Lena was expecting and prepared myself for a weekend of daddy-daughter time.

By the time Saturday rolled around I wanted to call Lucy and ask if she was really planning to come back, but that would be inappropriate. Right? But I needed to know that I could count on her to keep her word. I had important deals in the works that required me to be at the office, present and not distracted by thoughts of the nanny.

Instead of calling her, I sucked it up and finished the weekend doing full-time parenting duty. Lena and I spent an incredible weekend together, and I only thought about Lucy every thirty or forty seconds or so.

It was a good weekend, but I was off my game and Lena could sense that something was wrong even if she never asked about it. She was quiet and obedient all weekend, which only made me feel like a terrible father on top of an asshole.

On Sunday, I finally managed to pull my shit together enough to act normal in front of my daughter. We ate breakfast and chatted about the week ahead, which consisted of conversation about Lucy. The things Lucy said and did, words of wisdom she'd imparted, and even all the reasons Lena loved her nanny. It was maddening even if it was heartwarming to know I'd finally done something good in finding an excellent caregiver for my daughter.

When Lucy finally arrived back at the mansion late that afternoon I felt like my old self again. Mostly. I managed a smile. Okay, it was a grin, but it felt genuine and believable.

But she didn't speak to me even to greet me, she just hugged Lena before she carried her bag upstairs and she remained in her suite for the rest of the evening.

It really was time, beyond time, to apologize.

Chapter 27

Lucy

Sunday afternoon arrived far too soon for my liking. After a relaxing weekend spent mostly in total silence, coming back to the mansion felt like a foreign country. It had only taken a few hours to get used to roaming around the living room, cooking meals for myself, not to mention a very distinct lack of Dante Rush. And before I knew it, the calendar had flipped to Sunday and it was time to get back to work and get ready for the week ahead.

I returned to the mansion with a bag of clean laundry along with five meals prepped and ready to eat as is, or fresh from the microwave. It was all part of my plan to remain professional and keep my distance. I had meals, a case of water, a few cans of pop, and some snacks. It was just enough food to get me through the week without succumbing to the urge to join Lena and Dante for dinner.

A knock sounded at my door, and I could tell by the

softness of the tentative tap that it wasn't Dante, so I pulled the door open with a smile. "Lena. What's up?"

She looked left and then right before she leaned in and giggled. "You want to have dinner with us Lucy?"

Yes. "That is a very kind invitation, but I think you should enjoy dinner with your father before the week starts and he gets busy again. Don't forget to tell him how much you'll miss him and how much you love how hard he works for you." I spread my mouth into what I hoped was a believable smile and ruffled her hair. "Did you have a good weekend?"

"I did. Daddy took me to a puppet play and to a very fancy dinner. I got to dress up and it was so much fun!"

"That's great to hear, Lena. I'm so happy for you." Spending time with her father was good for her, especially since they were all each other had in the world. I would have given anything to have even a fraction of the attention from both of my parents that Dante managed as a single parent. "Don't forget to wash your hands before dinner!"

"I won't," she replied with a small smile before she ran off down the stairs and back to her father.

I smiled and shook my head before I closed the door and got back to putting my clean clothes away. I had seen Dante for a few moments when I first arrived and we hadn't exchange any words, not even a simple polite greeting. In fact, we hadn't said anything to each other in more than a week and it was both gratifying and torturous. It was the only way to move forward without things getting messy, no matter how awkward it was.

No matter how much it hurt.

It won't hurt forever, I reminded myself before I stepped into a steaming hot shower. The water pounded against my aching muscles and the steam opened my pores, relaxing me until I felt calm and thoughts of Dante no longer interrupted perfectly reasonable thoughts of everything else. Feeling refreshed and mostly ready to face the week, I stepped out of the shower and into the steamy bathroom with a half-smile on my face. I took my time as I applied leave-in conditioner to my hair, moisturizer on my skin and slipped into a pair of comfortable cotton pajamas.

Sometime after ten o'clock another knock sounded on the door, and this time I knew it was Dante. I inhaled a deep breath and let it out for as long as I could, steeling myself for an interaction with my boss. With another breath to strengthen my resolve, I gripped the doorknob and turned it slowly.

"Yes?" I ignored how good Dante looked, even in a pair of sweatpants and a t-shirt that clung to his sculpted muscles.

"Lucy." He opened his mouth and closed it, almost as if he was at a loss for words, something I was sure felt foreign to a man like Dante. "I think we should talk."

I folded my arms in an unconsciously protective gesture. "I don't think that's necessary. Is there anything I need to know about Lena?" Talking about what he said wouldn't solve anything, which meant it was pointless.

"Ah, no," he grunted with a sheepish grin. "I owe you an apology."

I shook my head and took a step back as if I could put some distance between me and whatever words he felt he needed to say. "No, you don't."

"I do." He stepped forward until he was inside my room and closed the door behind him. "I'm sorry that I was such an asshole the other day. I have no excuse, not for how I spoke to you or what I said, and, well I'm sorry."

"Fine," I stepped back again. "Apology accepted." The words didn't make me feel better, but I knew they wouldn't, so I slapped a smile on my face and nodded, pretending that his apology fixed everything.

"You don't mean that." His expression was serious, his body one tightly coiled mass of muscles and tension. "Dammit Lucy, what can I do?"

I sighed wearily. "What does it matter, Dante? You don't care, you just don't want things to be awkward."

"Damn right I don't!" His words rolled across the room and I wrapped my arms around myself.

With as much calm as I could muster, I nodded. "Things aren't awkward Dante, they're exactly as they should be. Professionally distant. We don't need to be friendly or share meals. We have one shared goal, and that's Lena's education and well-being, so that is what we need to focus on. Nothing else."

"And if I can't?"

I smiled though it didn't reach my eyes. "You can, and

if you can't, then remember that I'm looking to trade up to someone richer than you. That should make things easy."

He rolled his eyes. "So you don't forgive me?"

I shrugged. "There's nothing to forgive, Dante."

"Bullshit." He shook his head. "You're angry, so just say that you are."

I was furious. "I'm not angry. Why would I be?"

"Dammit Lucy, just be honest with me."

I sighed, doing my best to look bored. "I don't owe you honesty, Dante. I said I'm fine, so accept it or don't, I don't care."

Dante rushed towards me, closing the distance between us quickly until he was in my face. "I can see that you don't, but dammit I do care. I'm sorry, okay?"

"And I've already accepted your apology. What else do you want Dante?" I pushed at his chest. He was too close, his scent engulfed me and took over my senses. The warmth that radiated from his body heated my skin until I couldn't think straight.

"What I want Lucy," he growled and rested one palm on the wall behind me, "I can't have." The other hand went to the wall and locked me between his arms. "You."

A shaky breath escaped, but I couldn't say anything because Dante held me transfixed in his deep green gaze. I wanted to reject his words, to tell him that he didn't really want me. I wanted to say that it was because I was close by. Easy. But the moment I opened my mouth his lips were on mine, his tongue slipped between my lips and his hands gripped my waist. The kiss was sexier than the others. It contained a raw hunger that was irresistible.

Had anyone ever wanted me so desperately? Ever needed me like this? I didn't have to think about it, the answer was no, not ever. Not until Dante had any man needed me this way, or made me feel so needed, and I was powerless to do anything other than dive straight into the kiss and let it swallow me whole.

Dante kissed me like I was his whole world and I let him. No, that's not right, I didn't just let him, I leaned into the feeling and let it warm me down to my bones. Before I knew it I was falling to the bed and Dante was on top of me. His hands tore at my clothes while his mouth devoured mine. He moved from my mouth and down my body, kissing every inch of my skin until I felt as if I might die from the sheer pleasure of his lips on my flesh.

I arched into him as his shoulders pushed my thighs apart and he slicked his tongue through where I was hot and pulsing for him. I bit my bottom lip and gripped his hair tightly. "Yes."

Dante's tongue was pure magic and fire, hot and devilish as it rolled against my clit over and over like it was battery powered. He growled like I was a dish he couldn't get enough of, and he dove deeper, licked with greater intensity until pleasure exploded out of me like a volcano erupting after lying dormant for centuries.

The orgasm pushed fire through my veins and I gripped his hair tight, holding him close until every last inch of pleasure was wrung dry. "Mmm," I purred as my body went slack.

But Dante wasn't done yet. He placed a long, slow French kiss to my slit before he licked his way up my belly and back to my mouth, slipping inside of me in one long stroke. "Ah, yes. So, so good." He grunted his pleasure and held on tightly to me as he thrust deep, placing open mouth kisses on my neck and collarbone. "Lucy."

I kept my eyes close and just let myself feel. I didn't want to think, not about who was making me feel this good, or why it was such a stunningly bad idea. I just wanted to enjoy the physical intimacy, the sensual satisfaction that pulsed through my body, and that's what I did. "Yes," I moaned. "More."

He hooked his arms under the back of my knees and pounded harder into me, grunting in my ear before he nipped it. "Ah, fuck. Lucy!" His hips moved faster and his thrusts came deeper and with more intensity, the sensation was so good that my toes curled and a shiver stole down my spine.

It was so good, I felt tears gather in the corners of my eyes and squeezed them tighter, willing thoughts to go away so that there was only room for orgasms. "Yes," I moaned and bucked up to meet him thrust for thrust. "Dante, yes!"

His lips left my skin and he whispered in my ear. "Look at me Lucy."

Without a question my eyes opened and our gazes collided with a palpable intensity that sent a wave of discomfort through me. I didn't like this feeling at all, but I loved the way my body felt. "I see you Dante."

He smiled and his jaw clenched as his orgasm took over. "Lucy," he grunted and then slammed his mouth against mine. He kissed me long and hard, the friction of his cock pumping inside of me until I couldn't stand it any longer and my second orgasm crashed down over me. "Ah, fuck!"

His roar of ecstasy did something wild, it prolonged my orgasm and it was wild, almost animalistic as I twitched and pulsed and vibrated while he continued to fuck me. It was heaven and hell combined into one sensation that I never wanted to end. "Oh, yes!"

Dante's face twisted in erotic agony as he pounded pumped harder, groaning until he came deep inside me. "Ah, Lucy." His hips slowed but several long seconds passed before he stopped completely, prolonging our pleasure until we were both limp and satisfied. He rolled to the side and I moved slightly, making sure we didn't touch.

It was an odd stand to take, but I had to keep my distance after what had just happened, the feelings it evoked, I knew I needed emotional distance above all else. "That was...intensely satisfying."

Dante laughed. "It was a whole damn experience."

It was. Unfortunately. "You should go." Okay that was abrupt and kind of rude.

Dante sighed. "Is this some sort of payback?" He turned to face me, his fingertips drew circles on my stomach.

"No. But I'd rather you leave before your regret sets in. Again." The last thing I needed to hear while I still glowed from two delicious orgasms was how it was a mistake, and how it couldn't happen again. "Let's just leave it at what it is."

His expression turned thunderous. "So, what, there are no second chances with you?"

"A second chance to hurt and humiliate me? No." I tried to get off the bed, but Dante's grip pulled me back. "Dante."

"I said I was sorry. Doesn't that mean anything to you?"

My shoulders fell at the emotion in his question. "Yes, it does actually. I believe that you're sorry about what you said in front of Alex and Lena. That doesn't change the issue of regret though, does it?"

"Dammit Lucy, I never said I regretted it."

"No," I conceded, "you never said that. Or anything. But you don't want this, do you Dante?" I figured a guy like him was ashamed that he was attracted to the plump nanny, and I couldn't blame him. Not that I thought there was anything wrong with me, I liked myself just fine, but I'm sure a handsome wealthy man like him was used to dating executives, insta models, and probably a few heiresses as well.

"It isn't that simple, Lucy."

"But it is," I shot back and wrenched out of his hold to stand. "I'm a big girl Dante and I don't need you to lie to me." Damn tears started to fall and I kept my back to him. "Just please, leave."

There was so much tension in the room, and I felt the weight and heat of his stare on my back. Dante wanted to argue, but what was the point? He wasn't trying to convince me of anything. Despite the off-the-charts chemistry and the fact that we couldn't be alone together without getting naked, he didn't want this. Didn't want me.

"This conversation isn't over Lucy."

It was, he just didn't know it yet.

Chapter 28

Dante

I was up half the night because Lucy's words replayed in my head on a constant loop. She thought I regretted being with her, but that was a fucking joke. How could she think that when being with her was so incredible?

The truth was that being with Lucy, worshipping her curvy body and hearing the sounds she made when I gave her exactly what she needed was unlike any sexual experience I've ever had. I'm a red-blooded male who loves women and sex, and I loved using my skills to make a woman feel good. It was just how I was built. But with Lucy? It was a whole new ballgame. I didn't just want to please her, I *needed* to please her. The moment she was naked all I wanted to do was touch and taste every inch of her. Her soft cries and throaty groans kept me hard and fired up to see what new areas I could explore, what new sounds I could draw from her.

But a night of sleep hadn't produced any answers, at least none that would satisfy Lucy. So I kicked off the covers early and made my way down to the gym to work off some of this frustration. Running was an effective way to clear my head, so I started with a seven mile run, but when that didn't provide any answers, I grabbed the free weights and worked every muscle in my body until they screamed and finally I tapped out.

A hot shower didn't help either, because it only reminded me of the one and only shower I'd shared with Lucy. It hadn't just been sensual, it was an out of body experience.

As the hot spray rained down over me I closed my eyes, and there she was down on her knees and smiling up at me as she stroked my cock, flicked her tongue over the slit before she took me deep. She was everything I shouldn't want—bubbly and sweet and upbeat—and yet I wanted her, and not just in my bed.

I took my cock in hand, eyes still closed and stroked to the images of Lucy taking me deep as she hummed her own satisfaction at pleasing me. It took no time at all for long, thick streams of jet to fly against the shower wall. I finished quickly and went through my morning routine until I was dressed and ready for the day.

As ready as I can be with less than two hours of sleep.

"Good morning, Dotty." I made a beeline to the coffeepot and filled a mug before I gulped it down black.

"Rough night?"

I ignored the amusement in Dotty's tone and simply nodded. "Didn't sleep well."

"Good," she murmured to herself. "Something on your mind?"

"You could say that," I growled and refilled my mug, this time with sugar and cream. "What's for breakfast?"

"Breakfast sandwiches, requested by Lena. Biscuits, sausage and eggs with or without cheese." She smiled across the counter expectantly.

"Without cheese, thanks." I took my time on the second cup of coffee while Dotty made breakfast, the fatty scent of sausage wafted in the air.

"My goodness Dotty, it smells incredible in here. Are those biscuits?" Lucy entered the kitchen with Lena's hand in hers, wide blue eyes filled with excitement. "You're a goddess, Dotty."

"Fresh biscuits for the sandwiches Lena requested."

"Thank you, Dotty." Lena rushed to the housekeeper and wrapped her in a hug before she pulled back with a smile and rushed to the table. "Morning Daddy."

"Good morning, Lena. How are you feeling?"

"Good."

The doorbell rang and Dotty sighed, her gaze shot from the sausage patties on the stove to the direction of the door. "Are we expecting company?" She asked with a sigh.

"I'll get the door," Lucy offered. "You focus on breakfast."

"Bless you, Lucy."

She laughed. "Just remember me when you're adding cheese to the biscuit sandwich."

"Well look at you," a familiar voice said. "Even prettier in person."

Lucy's laugh sounded loud and genuine. "I could say the same about you, Sam. Cheryl, you're looking youthful. Come on in."

I sat taller and set my coffee down just as Lucy entered the kitchen with my parents close behind her. "Mom. Dad. This is a surprise." They hadn't called or mentioned anything about a visit, which immediately put me on edge.

Mom laughed and moved forward to wrap me in a suffocating hug. "It's good to see you too, Dante."

"You look good, Mom. Dad you look...tan."

Dad laughed and pulled me in for a back-slapping hug before I could even get to my feet. "Sunshine is good for the soul, my boy. Looks like you could use some, you're as tense as a corpse."

Dotty laughed from her spot at the stove.

"Grandma! Grandpa!" Lena slid from her chair and rushed to my parents excitedly. "You're here!"

It was a minutes' long love fest as Mom and then Dad hugged and kissed Lena, and chatted about how happy they were to see each other. "You've gotten so big!" Dad lifted Lena high in the air and she giggled.

"What're you doing here?" The question was abrupt and harsh, which wasn't how I meant it.

Lucy laughed, but tried to stifle it with a cough. "Need

some help Dotty?"

"Sure. Let's just do family style."

I watched Lucy as she brought a plate of biscuits to the table followed by more plates and silverware to accommodate my parents. Coffee mugs came next followed by maple syrup and strawberry preserves. "All right, is everyone set?" She surveyed the table like a professional and flashed a smile at my parents.

"We're good, honey." Mom flashed a smile and looked around the table with a frown. "You aren't eating breakfast with us?"

"No," she said and maintained her bright but professional smile. "You guys should catch up over breakfast. Just give me a call when you're done and I'll come grab Lena, unless I should stay to help her?"

"Oh no," Dad insisted. "We can handle one little squirt." He winked at Lucy and she smiled in return.

I watched her walk away powerless to stop her, equally powerless to make her stay. "What?"

Mom stared at me as if she wanted to say something. Instead, her lips curled into a knowing grin. "Nothing. How are you, son?"

"I'm fine, Mom. Working a lot and spending the rest of my time with Lena. How are you guys?"

"Good. Missing our son and granddaughter," she answered and tickled Lena. "Figured we'd swing by for a visit before you could tell us you were too busy."

"I wouldn't," I began, but stopped. "Okay maybe I would, but I'm glad to see you." Things at work were incredibly busy, especially today. "But I'm afraid that I can't skip work today. Tomorrow, however, is all yours."

"Perfect. Today we'll hang with Lena, maybe take her to the zoo, if that's all right."

"Of course it is. I'll let Lucy know."

"Let Lucy know what?" She appeared as if I'd conjured her up, smiling in skintight jeans and soft pink tunic.

"We're taking Lena to the zoo," Mom announced. "Would you like to join us?"

Her gaze slipped to mine and then back to Mom. "I'm happy to tag along if you need help with Lena, otherwise I think she would enjoy spending time with you guys on her own."

Mom looked as if she wanted to say more, but she surprised me when she held her tongue and nodded. "Maybe another time."

"I'll get you the keys for the Escalade. The car seat is already installed along with everything else Lena might need for a car trip." She smiled sweetly at my parents before she turned to leave the kitchen again.

"Sounds good," I told my parents. "Tonight we'll all go out to dinner. You too, Lucy."

She froze at my words and turned slowly, a stormy expression flashing on her face briefly. "Fine, ok, thanks." She turned to Lena and my parents with a smile. "Have fun today!" She spun and left for real this time. Quickly.

"That was interesting," Mom said, her voice filled with curiosity.

"I have to agree," Dad said with a laugh as his gaze swung to mine.

"No, it's not," I said and stood abruptly. "I need to get going."

Mom and Dad erupted in laughter as I kissed them all and rushed out the door before they started asking questions.

Chapter 29

Lucy

"Y ou look beautiful Lucy." Dante's mom beamed at me like it was my prom night.

I looked down to see if I was overdressed. I wasn't sure where Dante planned to take his family, but it was a sure bet the place would be fancy, and by extension expensive. I opted for a plain navy blue dress that highlighted my curves without making me stand out.

"Am I dressed all right? I wasn't sure where we were going."

"Oh honey, you are dressed perfectly. Such a knockout, isn't she Dante?"

My hands balled into fists at my side, but that was my only concession to Dante's presence. I told myself that it didn't matter what he thought about me or my appearance.

"Lucy looks gorgeous as always."

My skin heated at his seemingly sincere compliment, damn him. "Thanks," I muttered and turned away. "I need to help Lena." It was a weak excuse, but it happened to be true, so I made my escape. "Hey Lena, need some help?"

She nodded. Her curly pigtails swung with the move.

She looked so distraught that I couldn't help but smile at her small face. "Let's find you a dress. What color do you feel like wearing?" I took her hand and led her to the closet, filled with more clothes than a four-year-old girl would need before her next growth spurt.

Lena tapped her chin deep in thought before she stepped forward and touched a pale purple dress and then a deep pink one. "This one?"

"It's beautiful," I told her honestly. Lena's clothes were perfect for any stylish little girl, colorful and flattering and adorable. "Now you need shoes."

She picked out shoes and then tights and I helped her get dressed and fixed her hair.

There was nothing else to be done, which meant I'd exhausted all of my stalling tactics. We piled into another SUV—not the Escalade—and I jumped in the back, as far away from Dante as possible. His father took the front passenger seat while Lucy and Cheryl sat in the middle.

I didn't belong and I refused to pretend anymore. It was a lesson I was determined not to forget.

But I planned to enjoy every delicious morsel of the food served at the upscale steakhouse Dante took us to somewhere in the heart of Houston. We were shown to a round table and I sat beside Lena to help her, because that was my role here, nanny. Not friend and not family.

Employee.

I played the role of observer for the night, watching everything, and what I saw made it harder to *want* to keep a physical and emotional distance from Dante. He was grumpy because that was his default setting, but he was also charming and affectionate with his parents, just as he was with Lena. There was an easy affection between all four of them, they touched freely and easily, laughed together, and teased each other good-naturedly.

It was a nice side of him to see, or at least it would have been if I wasn't so determined not to care. I shouldn't have had sex with him—again—last night. It was a mistake, even if it was the most enjoyable, satisfying mistake of my life. The things he made me feel terrified me because it was deeper than sexual satisfaction. It was more than chasing orgasms, more than satisfying a physical need, and it was that *more* that I refused to address.

"So Lucy, tell us about yourself." Cheryl's question pulled me not just from my reminders to stop thinking about her son, but from my role as silent observer. "Where're you from?"

I put a smile on my face and turned to Cheryl. "I'm from Georgia, a town just outside Atlanta."

"A southern girl," Sam said with a smile. "That explains why you're both sweet and sassy, just like my Cheryl." He looked at his wife with such affection my heart lurched a little and I had to look away.

"Are you single?"

"Mom," Dante growled. "That's Lucy's personal business."

I frowned. Why did he care? "I am. Very single and no plans to change it anytime soon." I smiled at the slight frown on Dante's face at my words.

Cheryl leaned forward with sympathy in her eyes. "A recent bad break up?"

"Sadly, no. It's hard to meet people in my line of work. Most of the people I spend time with are parents and small children, so no dating prospects, and when I'm free on the weekend I run errands, clean or just chill out."

"You don't go out in the evenings?"

The more I talked, the more pathetic I felt. "Not lately. This assignment is a little farther away from the city, so it doesn't make sense to drive so far and return too late to get a good night's sleep." Yep, sad and pathetic about summed it up. "What about you two, how long have you been married? You seem like newlyweds."

It was the perfect question, because it allowed me to slink back into oblivion while hearing all about the love story of Cheryl and Sam. The retelling of which had the added benefit of making Dante uncomfortable.

"It was lust at first sight, but I held on long enough to get her to fall in love with me." Sam concluded with a chuckle.

"What a wonderful story!" It gave me hope that I would someday find what they had together, even if that day was so far into the future that it wasn't on any calendar yet.

"Daddy doesn't have a girlfriend," Lena said completely out of the blue.

Dante's brows dipped into a frown. "What do you know about girlfriends?"

She giggled. "All princesses have a boyfriend before they become princesses, Daddy."

I smiled to myself as conversation swung from me to Dante and his nonexistent love life. Mr. Unflappable was in the hot seat and I enjoyed every single moment of his discomfort.

Until talk turned to him finding a wife.

Talk about swift karma.

Chapter 30

Dante

"You can't avoid me forever Lucy."

A midnight trip to the kitchen for a bottle of water brought me face to face with the woman who'd gone out of her way to avoid me. My parents had been in town for the past four days and Lucy had used their presence to keep a wide gulf between us.

Lucy turned with an arched brow and stared at me, an amused smile curled up her one side of her mouth. She folded her arms, the cotton tank top did fuck all to cover her the way her tits nearly spilled over the top.

"Good because I'm not avoiding you."

"Really? Because it sure feels like you're going out of your way to avoid me." She made sure we were never alone, and if we came close to being alone, Lucy found a reason to get gone.

She shrugged like it was no big deal. "Believe what you want, but I'm not avoiding you. I have no reason to avoid you since we have no reason to talk." She licked her lips and let out a long, slow exhale. "Is there something I need to know regarding my care of Lena?"

I wanted to growl my frustration loud enough to wake the far-flung neighbors, but there was no point, because Lucy had decided we had no reason to interact if it wasn't about my daughter. She wasn't wrong. Weeks ago, that exact sentiment would have been music to my ears. Today it just pissed me off.

"You know there isn't," I growled. "You're doing a fantastic job with her."

Her blond brows dipped in confusion. "Then what is the problem?" She was clearly oblivious to the way her gorgeous breasts spilled over and made my mouth water.

I took a few steps closer. "You know damn well what the problem is!" The truth was I didn't even know what the hell the problem was. I had been less than definitive with what I wanted where Lucy was concerned, and unlike most women who were content to go along to get along, she'd called me out and refused to budge an inch.

"No, I don't." She sighed and shook her head. "What does it matter, and more to the point, why do you even care? I am doing exactly what you—and men like you—want me to do. I'm pretending it didn't happen to make both our lives easier."

"I know! You're right, it *is* exactly what I thought I wanted, but it turns out I have no fucking clue what I want."

Something that resembled hurt flashed in her eyes

before she recovered. "Well we both know that what you want isn't me, so maybe you should do as your mother suggested and go find someone suitable for your lifestyle. Someone you know isn't using you for your money, or your...whatever."

Her fiery words should have worried me, but I just smiled. "My whatever?"

Lucy shrugged. "Yeah. I'm sure there're wannabe models or fashion designers out in the world happy to share your bed in hopes of becoming the next big thing in fashion. A few nights in your bed can catapult them to superstardom. Go find them." She waved her hands in a shooing motion that would have made me mad if anyone else had done it.

From Lucy it was just charming. I took a few steps forward, closing the gap between us until I was close enough to see the varied shades of blue that darkened her gaze. "I don't want them Lucy. It turns out that I only want you."

She placed both her palms on my chest and shoved until I fell back a few steps. "That is a damned lie Dante and you know it!"

The pain that stabbed my heart at her words was palpable. She didn't believe me, and once again it was my own fault. "I don't say things I don't mean Lucy, not even to preserve anyone's feelings."

She rolled her blue eyes skyward. "Whatever." She tried to brush past me but I grabbed her shoulders.

"Lucy," I growled and spun her around until we were

chest to chest. My mouth crashed down on hers and I savored the taste of her, minty with just a hint of red wine. She tasted heavenly, and I slowed the kiss as my hands wandered down her back and gripped her round ass. Her curves filled my hands and I slowed my moves even more, determined to savor the taste of her before she came to her senses.

She moaned into my mouth and pushed in closer, leaning her head back while our tongues tangled together. In and out, my tongue penetrated her mouth the same way I wanted to lay her out on the counter and drive into her lush pussy.

Kissing Lucy in the kitchen was the best I'd felt all week, and that thought scared me. This should be about satisfying my desire for her, nothing else, and the idea that kissing her made me feel better was too much to bear. It scared the hell out of me to think of Lucy as something more than satisfying a physical need, but I couldn't have pulled away from her under the threat of death.

Too soon though, Lucy pulled back with swollen lips and a glazed look in her blue eyes. There was defeat and sadness in her tone when she spoke to me. "Dante you can't keep doing this."

"I know." I agreed with her that I couldn't keep doing this, couldn't go on like this. It wasn't as if I wanted this, but that didn't matter. "I know Lucy, but I can't stay away."

"This isn't fair. You don't want me, not for who I am, but because I'm convenient. I'm here, footsteps down the hall from you, which makes me the perfect woman for you. Right. Now." She shook her head and let out a sigh that held the weight of the world. "I don't have casual sex, Dante. Not really, and I'm honestly not built for it. If you, no, if *we* keep this up I'm the one who is going to get hurt. So please, please stop this." She motioned between us as tears swam in her eyes.

I wanted to tell her that she was wrong. I wanted to promise that I wouldn't hurt her, but I couldn't be sure that wouldn't happen. I was rusty at dating and romance, and my marriage was proof that I wasn't cut out for the long term either. So, when Lucy shoved my chest I reluctantly stepped aside and let her go.

For now.

I watched her walk away, and thankfully this time she didn't rush away from me, she just walked slowly and deliberately as if she might break down before she made it to her room. My heart was in my chest as she put more and more distance between us until I turned away and grabbed a beer from the fridge.

She was right, it wasn't fair, not to either of us. But that didn't change how I felt, or how badly I wanted her.

A familiar slow shuffle sounded behind me and I knew without even looking that it was my dad. "What's all the commotion down here?"

I sighed. "Got into an argument with Lucy, that's all."

My dad's hand landed on my shoulder. "Are you in the habit of fighting with your nanny? I mean what in the hell would you even have to fight about? She's very competent, better than anyone you've ever hired before."

"Things," I answered with a half-laugh. "I can't seem to get a damn thing right when it comes to her."

"Your mother was right. There *is* something going on between you two. She spotted it damn near right away." He sighed. "So, what's the problem?"

"I wish I knew." That was lie. I knew. "Something happened and I didn't react well, or I don't know, the way she expected me to act."

"Why? Are you scared, or did you get what you wanted from her and you're trying to find your way out?"

"Wow, Dad. Don't pull any punches." He was a straight shooter ,and I braced myself for his next words of wisdom.

"I won't," he sighed again. "You know that. But whether I'm hard on you or not, your feelings for Lucy aren't going anywhere. You have to face them or risk losing her forever."

"I know. But there are reasons, good reasons, that we shouldn't be together. For starters, she works for me."

"And? You work so much Dante, where else are you going to meet a nice woman?"

"You have all the answers, don't you Dad?"

"No. Not all of them, but I think you should talk to Lucy and tell her how you feel. Women like to hear the words, they need to hear them. Men, well let's just say we have a tendency to send mixed signals."

Like making Lucy believe I didn't want her but still

fucking her every chance I got. "Dammit." Dad was right, I needed to fix things with Lucy, and that meant being honest. "Thanks Dad. For everything."

"Anytime, son." Dad clapped me on the back and walked out of the kitchen with a soft laugh. "Good luck, Dante."

"Thanks, Dad." I laughed myself, because I had a feeling I would need more than luck to smooth things over with the feisty nanny.

Chapter 31

Lucy

The quiet at Toni's place didn't feel oppressive, it felt like freedom as I walked around in nothing but a t-shirt and cotton panties, a pair of wool socks covered my feet as I skated across the hard wood floors. There really was a difference between being alone and lonely. After a long week of keeping my distance and putting on a good show for Dante's parents, alone time was just what I needed.

I spent Friday evening *not* out painting the town red and drinking too much, instead I did laundry, stocked the fridge and made a big pot of stew and a loaf of sourdough bread. It was a relaxing evening and I only thought about Dante, oh about five times every hour. It was progress though, and today I was determined to beat that record.

My phone rang and I picked it up without looking at the screen since I'd already dodged calls from my parents and my sister. "Hey Toni."

She laughed in response. "Are you bored out of your mind yet?"

"Absolutely not! I have clean clothes, a clean living space and a big pot of stew and a fresh loaf of bread to eat. What are you up to?"

"Oh, nothing much, just hiding from a nerdy gamer who I'm pretty sure hates my guts."

I frowned. "What? How is that even possible?" Toni was tough and she was also a smart ass, but she was great.

"Bad taste?" She laughed and I closed my eyes, leaning back on the sofa. I could almost see her laughing. "Are you okay Luce? You don't sound like yourself."

"I'm fine," I assured her. "Or I will be. My heart isn't broken or anything, but I'm just sick of not being enough, you know? It's not like I was expecting Dante to propose or fall in love with me or anything, but I also wasn't expecting whatever the hell this was."

"I know, and it does suck, but Lucy you have to know that it's his loss."

"Maybe." A knock sounded on the door and I frowned. "Did you send me something?"

"I would have if I'd thought about it. Open the door, and if it's a stripper text me sixty-nine. If it's an axe murderer, scream and I'll send the police."

I laughed and reluctantly got off the sofa. "You have quite the imagination Toni."

"You should see what I come up with during naked times," she laughed.

A quick look through the peephole and I gasped. "It's Dante."

Toni sucked in a breath. "What? Why? What does he want?"

"I don't know," I whispered. "I haven't opened the door."

"Well open the door!" she shouted over the phone.

I gave myself ten seconds of deep breathing before I pulled open the door. "Dante, is Lena all right?"

He smiled and my knees wobbled. "She's fine. These are for you." He shoved a bouquet of flowers at me with the smoothness of old sandpaper.

"What did he bring you?" Toni's tinny voice echoed and I rolled my eyes and raised the phone to my ear.

"I'll call you back Toni."

She laughed again, loudly. "Alright, I want all the details."

"Goodbye Toni." I ended the call and turned my gaze back to Dante, standing in the hallway with an uncertain expression on his gorgeous face. "Dante. What're you doing here?"

He sighed and then he smiled and sighed again. "Can I come in? Can we, ah, talk?"

Everything within me screamed no, told me to shut the door in his face and wait until Monday to deal with him. But when he stood there looking all beautiful and vulnerable, I couldn't deny him. "Yeah, sure. Come on in." I took a step back and waved him inside.

Dante looked around Toni's place for a few moments

before he turned to look at me. "You're wondering why I'm here."

"I am."

He flashed a sexy grin and dropped down on the sofa. "I'm here for you Lucy."

My heart raced at his words. I wanted to believe them. Desperately. It's as if he was finally saying what I always wanted him to say. But, I was a big girl, and that kind of thinking was just fairytale nonsense.

"We talked about this, Dante."

He shook his head. "No, you talked and I listened. I didn't agree to anything." His gaze was serious and that stopped any joke that I might have spit out to ease the tension.

I nodded and leaned against the wall on the other side of the room, leaving a coffee table and another sofa between us. "All right," I sighed. "I'm listening."

"First I want to start with an apology, because I owe you that, and don't even think I'm apologizing for the incredible sex. I'm not."

"Good to know," I told him with a small smile.

He flashed a smile of his own. "You caught me off guard, a lot actually. Hell, maybe all the time if I'm being honest." Dante raked a hand through his hair with a long sigh. "I didn't know what to say, so I said nothing and let you believe the wrong fucking thing."

I folded my arms and arched a brow. "What is the right thing?"

"I like you Lucy, and clearly I want you. But it's been a

long time since I've done this with a woman and I'm horrible at it."

Dammit, why did he have to be so hot when he was being vulnerable?

"I know you wouldn't hit on Alex."

"You know that now, but at the time you honestly believed it."

He nodded. "I did, but it had nothing to do with you, I swear. You have to understand Lucy that very few women are attracted to me for me."

"You mean they don't like you just because you're gorgeous with a great body?" I found that hard to believe.

His grin split his face. "No. I mean sure that makes it easier to fuck me, but with my money and influence, those are always the main attractions."

"So you believe that's all you bring to the table?" I found that hard to believe too.

"No, but I think it's what most women want from me."

"Your ex?"

"Definitely. Only I didn't realize it until she got pregnant. She started spending money like crazy, and then it turns out, she hated being a mother. Didn't like the mess or the responsibility." He laughed. "Even my money wasn't enough for her to stick around."

Damn, that was terrible, and my heart went out to him. "So we're all guilty for her sins. Got it."

There was a flash of temper before Dante leaned back against the sofa. "No." He shook his head. "That's not it at all. Like I said, I'm bad at this and I can't seem to get it right with you Lucy. But I want to get it right. You're worth it."

I sighed heavily as my heart thundered inside of my chest at his words. No other words could have possibly touched me more than those three words. *You're worth it.* Had I ever been worth it to anyone in my life? The answer was a simple, no, I hadn't.

But here he was, Dante Rush, telling me that I was worth a guy like him making an effort to be better. "Dante." I didn't know what to say. My hands trembled and my legs wobbled as emotion clogged my throat.

"I know it's a lot to ask Lucy, believe me I do, but I think we work well together. We shouldn't, but we do."

"You mean we shouldn't because you're a world class grumpy jerk most of the time?" I moved around the living room and took a seat at the other end of the sofa with my back pressed against the arm so that I could look at him.

"I guess," he grunted.

I laughed. "And I'm entirely too chipper?"

"You can say that again."

I couldn't help it, I laughed again. "But you still want me?"

"I don't just want you Lucy, I need you. This isn't just sex, though that part is pretty great." His lips curled into a contagious grin.

"It is," I agreed honestly.

"But that's not all, Lucy. I need you to know that. I'm not sure what we will become or what we can become, but I'd like time to explore it."

Hell yes. "What does that mean?"

He smiled. "It means we spend more time together," he answered and scooted over to the middle sofa cushion. "Go on dates." He slid over a little more. "Sneak in kisses when we can." He slid over until he was pressed against my side. "Get to know each other." His hand cupped the side of my face as he lowered his mouth to mine and the kiss was so sweet it brought tears to my eyes. Within that kiss was a million promises, and my heart was hopeful that Dante wanted to fulfill them all. I slid onto his lap and speared my fingers through his hair, melting into his kiss and his touch.

"Dante." My words came out breathless and I pressed my forehead to his. "I want you too."

He huffed out a laugh and gripped my hips tight. "Good, because I want you right now, so fucking bad I'm not sure I'll last very long."

"As long as we both get what we need, I don't care. Let's go to the bedroom, Dante." He did and we stayed there for the rest of the night.

And a good part of the next morning.

Chapter 32

Dante

Lying in my bed in my home with Lucy was the best I'd felt in a long time. Sure, my career was rewarding and I treasured the time I was able to spend with Lena, but this right here with Lucy? It was just for me. Every inch of her warm, naked body was pressed against mine, one hand rested over my heart and I had never felt so relaxed. I hadn't felt this good since before I proposed to my ex-wife.

She was perfect for me in every way, and being with her for the past two weeks made me feel different. Better. I was still irritable, and that probably wouldn't change, but I felt different. Lucy wasn't just full of sunshine and rainbows, she was also a serious person with a deep intelligence that made the times between orgasms just as special. The sound of her laughter was the best thing ever, and despite being her "favorite grump" I went out of my way to hear that sound as much as possible.

"Your heart is racing pretty quickly, Mr. Rush." The good humor in Lucy's voice was punctuated by a husky laugh. "Something on your mind?"

I turned over so that my body covered hers and pressed my lips to that spot right behind her ear, the spot that made her shiver and arch into me. "Yeah, it's you Lucy. You're on my mind. Always."

She laughed again and massaged her fingertips into the nape of my neck as she tilted her head back to give me better access to her. "Yeah? Because I was just thinking about you too. You and your magical mouth."

The way she hummed her approval deep in her throat sent all the blood rushing to my cock. "I love these curves," I told her and kissed my way down her body, enjoying every inch of her soft skin. The dip in her waist, the soft flesh of her belly, the way her thigh muscles coiled under my touch. "I wish I had a full weekend, maybe a whole month, to worship them."

She purred her approval at my words and gripped my hair tight until I sat up and looked at her. "No one has ever said that to me before."

My brows threaded into a frown. "That can't be." I shook my head. It was completely unbelievable that there were men on this planet who got to experience all of this and didn't appreciate it.

"It is, trust me." There was something in her eyes, a mixture of sadness and affection that touched me in that spot buried deep in my chest. "You see me differently."

I shook my head. "No Lucy, I see you. Just as you are."

Her lips curled into a slow, sexy smile. "Dante."

I pressed my lips to her belly and made my way lower and lower until her soft thighs cradled my shoulders. "I'm sorry you've dated so many idiots Lucy, but I'm happy that you were free when you came to me."

"Sweet and grumpy," she purred when I parted her lower lips and blew a gust of air on her clit. "My new favorite combination. Better than peanut butter and chocolate."

"Peanut butter and chocolate," I murmured and slicked my tongue along her damp folds in one long stroke that had her leaning into me. "Sounds like a combination I can work with." I smiled as I teased her with my tongue, the sounds she made spiked my arousal, but my tongue refused to leave her sweet honey.

"Yes, Dante. Oh yes." Her fingers tangled in my hair as words of pleasure spilled from her lips and her hips rolled against me.

A soft, rapid knock sounded on the door. "Daddy? Are you in there Daddy?"

Lucy froze and then laughed. "Duty calls. Daddy."

I looked up and my nostrils flared as heat pulsed through my veins at her words. "It does." My shoulders slumped forward and I laid my head on her belly, giving her sweet pussy another swipe of my tongue before I pulled back. "Rain check?"

She nodded. "You go take care of Lena and I'll stay right here and take care of myself." Her hand slipped between her thighs, the sound of her fingers dancing in her slick heat made me want to forget all about everything else.

"Lucy," I growled.

She laughed again. "There's my grump. Go," she urged and shooed me out of the bedroom.

I found my discarded pajama pants on the floor and stepped into them.

"Um, Dante? You might want to cover up a little more." Lucy pointed her toes at my midsection and I looked down.

My dick was hard and it tented my pants. "I blame you."

Lucy laughed. "I'll take the blame, but you should cover up for innocent eyes."

I sighed and stepped out of my pants and into the boxer briefs beside them, then pulled my pajamas back on as well. "I'll be back. Soon."

"Hurry," she smiled. "Daddy."

I grunted and took a few steps back. "You're killing me, Luce."

She licked her lips. "I'll be here."

I smiled and shook my head before I slipped out of the bedroom to tend to Lucy. It was odd, having a woman in my bed in my home. I hadn't had a woman here since Bethany, and I found it difficult to shut off the man part of me to focus on the father part. "What's up Lena?"

"Is Lucy here?"

I nodded and guided Lena away from the bedroom

even though my thoughts were still inside that room. "I'm sure she's around here somewhere. What do you need?"

"I'm hungry Daddy."

I smiled and picked Lena up as we made our way down to the kitchen for breakfast and I knew my naked time with Lucy was on a temporary, but long pause. "Let's find some breakfast then. How do pancakes sound?"

"Yay!"

The next few hours were dedicated to parenting, and it wasn't until late afternoon before I found my way back to Lucy and her bed.

Chapter 33

Lucy

I t was official.

I was head over heels, goofy grin on my face, in love with Dante Rush. I suspected it for a few weeks now and I knew it was happening, but I'd ignored it. Told myself that it was too soon, and that Dante wouldn't welcome the sentiment. Oh sure, I knew he liked spending time with me and that we had *something*, but I wasn't sure about this level of feelings.

I wanted to tell him every single time I saw him. When he wrapped me in his arms and pressed his lips to mine, I wanted to whisper *I love you* in his ear. When I gazed into his handsome face as it twisted in erotic agony, I wanted to shout it on my orgasm.

But things have been going well, and I didn't want to mess with something that wasn't broken. Just as Dante had promised, we'd gone on dates and spent time together, just getting to know each other. I knew that his favorite food was lasagna, that he loved broccoli and hated asparagus. I knew that he'd wanted to be a professional soccer player and had started House of Rush as a run-of-the-mill textile company and pivoted to fashion based on the advice of a very famous fashion icon. Everything I learned about him only made me love him more.

And it was getting harder and harder to keep it to myself. But I had to, for just a little while longer.

Dante's arms circled my waist and he nuzzled my neck with a low growl. "Lucy. You smell good, babe."

Babe. Would I ever get sick of hearing that? I leaned back until my head rested on his shoulder and moaned. "Thanks. You feel good." The feel of his lips against my skin was almost too much to handle and then his hands tightened around me. "Dante." I turned and wrapped my arms around him. "Hi."

"Hey." He brushed a soft kiss against my lips and hummed his pleasure. "How's your day?"

"Better now. Lena's napping," I told him and frowned. "Which means you're home early."

He nodded. "I missed you." Another soft kiss that set my heart galloping like a wild stallion.

"I missed you too," I purred against his mouth. "What are you going to do about it?"

"For starters, this." His mouth descended on mine and the kiss was slow and intense, as if we had all the time in the world to make out like teenagers. His tongue teased me, slicking across my lips in a drugging back and forth motion that kickstarted my libido into overdrive. Finally his tongue parted my lips and our tongues danced together like we'd been doing this for years instead of just a few weeks.

The temperature rose either inside of my body, or the kitchen itself had gotten hotter, either way, the result was the same, I felt overheated. Hot and bothered. Needy to have more of Dante. Breathless, I pulled back with heavy eyelids and a slow smile.

"That's an excellent place to start."

With a growl, he lifted me in his arms and carried me out of the kitchen and up the stairs where we stalked down the hall and kicked open his bedroom door. He lowered me to my feet and quickly closed the door behind us before ridding me of my jeans, t-shirt, my bra and finally, my panties. "Fuck you're so beautiful Lucy."

My skin heated and flushed at his praise and the appreciative look in his eyes. "Dante." I reached for him and cupped one side of his face gently, my heart so filled with love for this man that I had to physically bite my jaw to stop myself from saying the words. "You make me feel beautiful."

He smiled and licked his lips when I started to undress him. "You're killin' me."

I smiled and took my time. "I love seeing you in your suit, but I love you in jeans even more." My breath hitched at my almost admission as I unfastened his pants and shoved them to the ground. "But you in nothing in at all is my absolute favorite."

Dante pressed against me until I was trapped between him and the bed for a long moment before we tumbled onto the soft mattress, wild and hungry for one another. We made love like wild animals, desperate for one another as if we'd been apart for decades rather than hours. We kissed everywhere slowly and then quickly, and then frantic as if the world was ending.

I took him in my mouth and made him roar his pleasure as he spilled onto my eager tongue. He licked me until I begged for release and then we were there, face to face as he slowly sank into me. "Yes," he hissed out and rested his forehead on my shoulder. "I can't get enough of you, Lucy."

My heart hammered at his words and I wrapped my legs around him tight, arching into every stroke as his hips moved faster and deeper. Something was going on with him, and though I was scared, I was also thrilled. This was a different version of Dante, wild and unhinged. Like he needed me, really and truly needed me. No one else, just Lucy.

I dug my heels into the back of his thighs and bucked up to meet him stroke for stroke. Too soon, that telltale tingle started in the space between my toes and slowly crawled up my body as if my lust was boiling over. Dante thickened inside of me, pressed against every sensitive inch of me. "Dante," I moaned and clung to him.

"Come for me, Lucy." He pulled back and his green

eyes penetrated down to my soul as he plunged deep, over and over again.

I couldn't look away. He was so handsome and the expression on his face made me feel truly loved for the first time in my life. He stroked deep and swirled his hips and yanked a powerful orgasm from me. "Dante," I cried out and he slammed his mouth against mine even as his hips moved even faster.

"Lucy," he growled and pumped harder as I came apart around him.

"I love you, Dante." The words came out on a whisper, soft but loud enough to be heard.

Surprise flashed in Dante's eyes, but moments later he came hard and he collapsed on top of me. I held him for long seconds because I felt scared and vulnerable, because he hadn't said anything in response.

I held him because I had a feeling it might be the last chance I got to do so. I closed my eyes and held him until he rolled over, and promptly fell asleep.

I sighed and rolled away as my heart broke all over again. I glanced over my shoulder at Dante's back as it rose and fell with the soft breathing that came with sleep. Tears pooled in my eyes that even though Dante made me feel like I was enough, like I was beautiful and cherished and loved, that even though he made me feel that way, Dante didn't love me.

I slipped from his bed and dressed quietly, fleeing to the solitude of my own shower where I could let my tears fall in peace. I was in love with Dante and he didn't love me back, which gave me two choices.

Take what I could get and let it be enough.

Or leave.

By the time I stepped from the shower and wrapped a towel around myself, I knew what I would do. It was what I'd been doing my whole life.

I would let it be enough.

Chapter 34

Dante

Dammit. I heard Lucy when she said she loved me. The words had shocked me at first. But on the heels of that came a familiar warmth I thought I would never feel again. No, that's not true. This was unlike anything I've ever felt. It wasn't like the love I had for Lena, it was entirely different. And it was nothing at all like the love I thought I'd had for my ex.

Lucy's love made me feel like I was different. Like I was a better version of myself, funny and interesting. Kind. Hell, she even found my grumpiness entertaining. All that she made me feel, but when it came down to hearing the words, I froze.

Even though my back was to her, I felt her gaze on me. I felt her imploring me, pleading with me to turn around and say something. To say anything. Instead of doing any of that, I feigned sleep and let her leave my room.

I'd just gotten her back, and this time I was worried

there would be no forgiveness. Her words had shocked me but they weren't unwanted. Sure, I had worried about us, about the viability of our relationship, but every single night when she came to me or when I found myself at her door, everything was right with the world. Together we were incredible and explosive, unlike anything I have ever experienced. Together, we were perfect.

Go to her.

My conscious urged me to get out of bed and go after Lucy. To say the words she wanted, no, the words she *deserved* to hear. There was no doubt that I felt the same way, so why hadn't I said the words? More importantly, was I willing to let Lucy go because I was too damn scared to admit how I felt?

No.

After a shitty night of tossing and turning, I woke up early and went straight to the home gym where I pushed my body until I was covered in sweat. I ran on the treadmill until my legs screamed at me to stop. I pushed every muscle until I ached. But still, my mind hadn't settled and I was no closer to a plan to tell Lucy how I felt.

A long, hot shower still hadn't produced any answers but at least my sore muscles felt a hint of relief. It was time to get some help. I grabbed my phone and called the one person who would give it to me straight.

"Dante," Alex laughed, sounding like he'd been up for hours despite the early hour. "Didn't know you suits got out of bed before nine o'clock."

"Funny. Is this a good time?"

"That depends," he answered with a smile in his voice.

"On what," I barked. My patience was already thin and I knew Alex was having too much fun at my expense.

"On what you're calling for. Are you calling to tell me that you screwed things up with the hot nanny?"

I said nothing, just stared at the phone with enough anger to explode the damn thing.

"I'll take that as a yes," Alex said, his tone smug and self-satisfied. "Tell Uncle Alex how you fucked up."

A reluctant smile parted my lips. "You're not my uncle."

"Details. You want my help or not?"

I pinched the bridge of my nose. "Honestly? I'm not sure."

Alex barked out a laugh. "That's fair, but you *did* called me."

He was right, of course. I inhaled deeply and as I exhaled, I told Alex everything about my relationship with Lucy from the beginning until last night. "And that's about it." I held my breath and waited for Alex to hit me with a brilliant idea that would guarantee I didn't lose Lucy. At the very least, I expected him to mock me.

"You forgot one thing," he offered up after a long, torturous silence.

I frowned even though he couldn't see me. "What's that?"

"The part where you love her too, only you're too chickenshit to tell her."

"That's why I'm calling you, Alex. I messed up by not saying it back in the moment."

He laughed. "You mean pretending you were asleep so you didn't have to deal with it."

"Yeah, that," I grunted, annoyed at his blunt yet accurate assessment of my behavior last night.

"You love her." It wasn't a question because Alex knew me well.

"I do. I love her man, but I thought I was in love once before and remember how that turned out. It nearly ruined my life."

"Wow, you're not just a scared little bitch. You're a coward." Alex laughed. "I'm surprised."

"You're not helping."

"I am. You just don't like the way my help is delivered." He let those words settle before he spoke again. "Lucy isn't Bethany. Lucy takes care of kids for a living, which means she's unlikely to up and decide she doesn't want motherhood. And she already said she loves you so what's the problem?"

"She's young. Feelings change."

"And you're old. Feelings still change. What the fuck does that even mean?"

I sighed. "It means she might want me now, but she's young and I don't want to get my heart broken again."

"Bullshit. Your heart wasn't broken when Bethany left, your ego was bruised, which is damn hard to do for an ego that size," he laughed. "You liked Bethany and the

211

image of you two together, it was never love. This is different, it's why you're so terrified."

"You're right." The moment the words left his mouth, I knew they were true. I hadn't even been nervous on my wedding day, because marrying Bethany was the right move. "So, what do I do?"

"That's easy," Alex said confidently. "You have to go big."

"Big. Like a big diamond?"

"No," he laughed. "Although that might work too, but Lucy isn't really that kind of woman, is she?"

"No," I confirmed.

"Didn't think so. I mean you need to make a big show of telling her you love her. If you can't do that, be prepared for some other man to snatch her up. Women like that don't stay single long, Dante."

Just the idea of another man being in Lucy's life and having the right to touch her made my hands clench in anger. It was a repulsive thought, one I couldn't tolerate.

"She's mine," I growled.

"Then go get her."

I stood and looked around the room, for what, I had no idea. "I will."

"Excellent. I would love to help, but I need to shave a few milliseconds off my forty. These fucking new kids coming up move like lightning." His tone was playful but I knew it was the truth.

"Want me to create some super light gear for you?"

"Fuck you," he laughed. "But I don't *not* want you to create exactly that."

We shared a laugh. "I'll talk to R&D and you go practice. Thanks for listening, Alex."

"Always. I expect to be Best Man, so don't fuck it up." He laughed again before the line went quiet. "Good luck, Dante."

"Thanks. Back at you." I ended the call with a renewed sense of purpose.

I loved Lucy, I knew that much, which meant I needed to come up with a way to not just tell her, but to ask her to stay with me and Lena.

Forever.

Epilogue ~ Lucy

Six Months Later

"Dante," I moan, arching into the touch of his lips against my breast as the sun streaked across the sky just outside our bedroom window. His mouth is doing delicious things to me, starting with my breasts. His tongue swirls around my nipple in concentric, drugging circles before he tugs on my nipple with a groan. "Yes, Dante."

He took my breast in his mouth as my legs wrapped around his big, strong body and my fingers speared through his hair. He groaned and switched breasts before he released me with a pop. "Lucy, babe. I can't get enough of you."

His grunted words tugged a smile across my face and I licked my lips, accepting the loving swipes of his lips, the gentle tug of his mouth on my flesh.

"You don't have to," I moaned and held him close. "I

want you. I always want you." It was the truth. Six months in and we couldn't get enough of each other, couldn't stop touching each other. If I had a free moment then I wanted to spend it with Dante. If he wasn't around, I counted down the moments until he was around.

It was an addiction that I couldn't shake and didn't want to. Dante was the only fix I needed and I leaned into it with everything I had. "Lucy." My name came out in a slow, strained groan as he slipped inside my core, pleasing me in long, slow strokes that took me out of myself.

Every invasion by his body was welcomed. Every long, deep stroke made me a part of Dante in the best way. He was buried so deep inside me, in my soul, that I knew nothing could separate us. "Lucy, babe."

My pleasure grew and spun out of control. I felt like a tornado growing and growing until my limbs were no longer my own, until my heart was the motivating force behind every move. "Dante," I moaned in warning as pleasure gathered in my toes and worked its way slowly up my body until I was like a bomb, ready to detonate with his next touch.

His mouth went to my neck and then my collarbone before he took my nipple in his mouth, tugging long and slow, it was the button that flipped the switch, pleasure flowing through my veins and out of my pores.

It was magical.

It was everything.

It was heaven on earth.

His hands roamed my skin as I fell back to Earth, his

mouth on my overheated skin until I landed safely back onto our bed. Satisfied, smiling and happier than I've ever been.

Dante's pleasure came moments later, the hot and hard length of him pumped and spilled into me. It was the perfect lazy Saturday morning, and I never wanted it to end. His body tensed and then collapsed with pleasure. "Lucy!"

I laughed nervously and held on to him as his pleasure ebbed. "Good morning to you too, honey."

He laughed, staying right where he was, buried deep until his cock slipped from me. "Great morning, babe. Love you." He smacked a kiss to my mouth and rolled to his side.

"Love you more," I moaned, my lips split into a permanent grin as I thought of the surprise I had for him today. "I need a shower."

"I'll join you," he insisted and did just that.

We enjoyed a long, erotic and leisurely shower that would make environmentalists angry, before we dressed and headed downstairs for breakfast. Dotty made my favorite, pancakes and sausage and eggs for breakfast. It was the perfect meal to boost my courage to reveal my secret. We left Lena with Dotty in the kitchen and I convinced Dante to head back upstairs where it would be more private after we'd eaten.

"What's on your mind, Lucy? It must be serious."

I frowned at Dante' question. For the past few months as we've gotten to know each other and settled into our new roles as a couple and joint caregivers, he seemed to know me better and better. Some days it felt as if he knew my thoughts before I did. "Who said there's something serious on my mind?"

He smiled. "I do. Talk to me, babe. What's up?"

I inhaled deeply, releasing it on a slow smile as the butterflies in my belly settled. "I have something to tell you, Dante. It's important, and serious."

His smile slipped and he gripped my hands in his. "You can tell me anything."

"I'm pregnant," I blurted out because I didn't know how else to share the news with him. I wasn't sure if Dante would be on board with growing our family since we hadn't really talked about it. Lena was thrilled that we were one big happy family, but our future was uncertain. "Dante... say something."

He blinked and continued to stare at me as if I spoke a foreign language. "You're pregnant."

"I am," I said slowly, warily. "How do you feel about that?"

Dante barked out a laugh and pushed off the bed. My heart pounded as I watched him disappear into his closet and wondered if he would return fully dressed before he asked me to leave. "I wasn't sure if you would want this, so I've been hanging on to it, waiting for the right time." He held up a black velvet box and jumped on the bed once again.

"The right time for what?"

"For us," he said and pressed a kiss to my bare belly.

'The right time to talk about our future. I know we've been playing things by ear, enjoying our happy bubble, but the future is ours and it's out there waiting for us to grasp it."

"Our future," I hummed. "That sounds nice."

"I'm glad you think so, because our future, you and me growing old together is all I've been able to think about for months, Lucy." He popped open the velvet box to reveal an over-the-top diamond ring that sparkled so bright it damn near blinded me. "Lucy, my sunshine. My love. Meeting you was the most unexpected moment in my life. Blond and bubbly and sassy, you were everything I didn't know I needed or wanted in this world."

I laughed. "You mean you weren't sure about a woman who told you off on the side of the road?"

He joined in on the laughter. "No, but every moment after that put us on the path to where we are today. In love, and ready to expand our family. You make me so happy, and I'm pretty sure I make you happy too?"

"Deliriously happy," I assured him with a soft kiss to his beautiful mouth.

"Perfect, because, I love you and I want nothing more than to start the rest of our lives together. Lucy, will you be my wife? My partner in life and in mischief?"

"In mischief? There's no way I can say no to an offer like that!" Life with Dante and Lena was never boring, that much was for sure. "Yes Dante, I would very much like to marry you and spend our life together in mischief."

"I promise you it's going to be a great life, Lucy."

I held the side of his face because he was the greatest

treasure I ever found in my life. "I have no doubt, Dante. It's already been so great.

"Remember you said that because I have one more surprise for you." He darted from the bed once again and returned with a large—no, a very large—garment bag.

"Um, what is that?"

He unzipped it slowly, nervously and turned to me as the silky white fabric was revealed. "It's for you."

"It's a wedding dress!" This man, so sweet and so considerate. "You bought me a wedding dress?"

"No. I had a wedding dress made for you. Don't you recognize it?"

The more I took in the beaded bodice, the flowing layers of tulle and silk, I did recognize it. It was a dress I had drawn when Lena and I were playing one day. The little girl had drawn her version of what her wedding dress would look like, complete with a cotton candy skirt, and she had begged me to draw my own. "You didn't."

He nodded. "I did. I told you Lucy that I want to be the one to help you make all your dreams come true. Even your dream wedding."

I sighed. "I've already got the groom of my dreams so what else do I need?"

"A wedding date. And to put that ring on your finger." He frowned and nodded towards the velvet box that rested in my palm.

I laughed and dramatically plucked the ring from its cushion and slid it onto my finger. "Looks nice. Big and sparkly." I looked up at him through my lashes and squealed. "We're getting married!"

"You're mine Lucy," he growled and knelt onto the bed. "Mine."

"Forever and ever," I promised with my whole heart. "I love you Dante Rush."

"And I am so in love with you, Lucy Lions."

He kissed me and we spent the morning getting started on our very own happy ever after.

THE END

A preview of Alex's story, Curvy Fake Wife for the Player is next!

Preview: Curvy Fake Wife for the Player

A too charming hockey player needs a marriage of convenience, and his curvy nanny is perfect for the role in this small town nanny romance.

Chapter 1

Alex

"I'm serious, Alex, you need to stay out of trouble. Just, I don't know, stay inside and have a beer, maybe watch a movie where a lot of shit gets blown up." I could hear the frustration and the seriousness in my agent, Jack's voice.

It was serious, I knew that, but I was Alex Witter, top winger for the Houston Highlanders, I didn't take anything too seriously except my career.

"I don't get into trouble, Jack. It just seems to find me." That was truer than I wanted it to be. "I just got back from visiting Dante, so you shouldn't hear anything about me other than I wore a feather boa while I had a tea party with a little girl." The trip to visit Dante had actually been fun and relaxing. The best part? Other than adoring fans, no one bothered me while I was there.

"That's good. Very good."

"Worried?" Jack had been my agent for nearly a

decade, I kept him on because he made me a very rich man with incredible endorsement deals and he always gave it to me straight, even the bad news. Maybe especially the bad news.

"Hell yeah, I'm worried. Top scorer in the League or not, another fuck up could cost you twenty million worth of endorsement deals. We have three contracts that renew this year, Alex."

Shit. "This is bullshit, Jack. I didn't force Tatiana to talk to the tabloids about our sex life." My ex, one of many, had hoped that her little stunt would get me to call her or rekindle our brief fling, or some such nonsense. She was dead wrong.

"Maybe so, but your name was connected to some acts most wouldn't consider family friendly."

"Yeah well I'm not a family man, am I?"

"No," Jack sighed. "You know how these morality clauses work, man. Keep your shit under wraps and stop fucking crazy."

I barked out a laugh at his advice. "Hard to do when you're me." It was how I always justified things that happened to me. But I took my job on the ice completely seriously, *and* the privileged life it gave me. "I won't do anything to screw up my business, but I can't be responsible for what other people do."

"You could stop sticking your dick in crazy, Alex. Training starts in a few weeks and I want you fresh and not distracted by anything. Feel me?"

I nodded even though he couldn't see me. "I feel ya, and I'll keep that in mind," I promised and ended the call.

I'd come too far in my life, from a dirt poor kid who grew up in a trailer park in Crayfish Hills, Tennessee to the number one high school, and then college prospect, before becoming the top scorer in the National Hockey League. I wouldn't let a spurned woman ruin it all because she wanted more than I ever promised her.

Fuck that. I loved my life. Some might consider it empty, the women and the parties, the vacations and the money, but it was exactly the life *I* wanted. The media called me *Hockey's Millionaire Playboy,* and to a certain extent, I played up the role for their sake. The fans ate it up, the women loved it too, and as long as I didn't go too far, management was fine with my antics. I made headlines both on and off the ice, and there had never been any problems with that.

Until now.

Fucking Tatiana. Jack was right about one thing, I had to stop sticking my dick in crazy before it caught up to me in a really bad way.

"I guess I'm staying inside," I said out loud to myself as I made my way to the kitchen, pulling a beer from the fridge along with a pack of steaks. My chef had left a few meals, but I was in the mood for something simple, so I seasoned the steaks, grabbed two more beers, and took the elevator to the roof. I lived in a penthouse apartment but the roof made it feel like a house with the grill area in one corner, plants and flowers all along the perimeter, and comfortable seating with a great view of all of Houston. Enjoying the last hour of sunshine of the day while I ate helped me relax. As much as I'd wanted to hunt down Tatiana and tell her off, I was glad my first instinct had been to call Jack. He'd gotten me a new phone number so she couldn't call, and planted stories that she was just jealous that I'd moved on before she did.

The truth was there was nothing to move on from. We met at a charity event and hit it off immediately, and by hit it off, I mean that we were instantly attracted to one another. She was interested and easy, which was exactly how I liked my women. I was interested and horny, and we'd spent a hot and adventurous week in bed together before we came up for air. We had our first date on day nine, and by day eleven I realized my mistake and broke things off with her. That was a year ago, and now that she was aging out of the modeling world, she was using me to stay relevant.

"Stop," I growled to myself as I finished off the steak and the second beer. She wasn't worth thinking about, but I gave in to a few more thoughts as I made my way back down to the apartment and then banished all thoughts of her from my mind completely.

I needed to focus on the upcoming season. I needed to be ready, to be sharp. There were always young players looking to steal my spotlight, and the closer I got to thirty, the harder the young bucks pushed. I wasn't ready to give up hockey yet, which meant I needed to focus. I grabbed another beer from the fridge, because when training started I would only indulge in alcohol on the weekends, and never more than two drinks until the season was over, which wouldn't be for a good long while if we made the playoffs for the sixth season in a row.

That third beer had knocked me on my ass, or maybe it was the sun and the stress. Whatever the reason was, I woke up to a moonlit sky. I didn't usually sleep in the middle of the day because there was always too much to do, but I'd been laying low since Tatiana's interview had brought the paparazzi vultures to my front door once again.

I rolled off the sofa to go in search of dinner, but a whimpering sound stopped me. I lived in a penthouse apartment so it wasn't as if there was a stray animal inside, but I went to check the roof since critters sometimes found themselves stuck up there. A quick look around revealed nothing, so I shrugged it off and went back downstairs.

The damn whimper sounded again and once again, I frowned. "What in the hell is that?" It sounded again and again, regular but not mechanical. I had no idea how a stray animal could have made it all the way up to my floor without being noticed, but the sound wouldn't quit so I opened the front door and froze.

A baby sat in a hot pink carrier on my doorstep. I looked up and down the hall, waiting for one of my players to jump out and take credit for this obvious prank, but there was no one there. No one but the whimpering baby kicking her chubby little legs in the air. "Where did you come from?" It was a good damn question but since the hall appeared to be empty, I had no choice but to pick up the carrier holding the baby and bring it inside.

I set the carrier on the kitchen counter and stared at the tiny thing with a shock of red hair and big green eyes. How did a baby end up on my doorstep? Mine was the only unit on this floor and it required a special key card to gain penthouse access. I picked up the phone on the wall that connected me immediately with the doorman. "Barry, has anyone been to my floor today?"

"No, sir. A few photographers tried to gain access but I got rid of 'em. Is there a problem?"

"I'm not sure yet. I'll let you know." I ended the call and turned back to the baby and the small bag hooked onto her carrier. There had to be some information on this baby somewhere. Right?

Inside there were a few diapers, baby bottles, and the smallest clothes I'd ever seen. Past the baby wipes and a tube of ointment was nothing except the bottom of the bag. "Dammit."

"Ba-ba-ba-ba." The baby babbled with a watery smile as she kicked her legs like she was trying to tell me something. She kicked again and that's when I heard it, the crinkle of paper.

Behind her kicking legs, I found a note.

Alex, I'd like you to meet your daughter. She has your eyes, don't you think? Before you curse me to hell and back, read this letter all the way through. She's yours and I have no doubts about that, but if you do, have a DNA test if you don't believe me.

Don't bother trying to track me down because I'll be dead by the time you find me, that's why I'm leaving her with you. Please, take care of our little girl, give her a good life and make sure she knows I loved her more than anything.

I know you don't think you have it in you to be a father, to be responsible for someone so tiny, but I know that you do. Take care of her, and yourself.

That was all the note said, she hadn't signed it or anything. A ball of acid formed in the pit of my stomach as the situation started to sink in. A baby. Someone had left a baby on my doorstep and said she was mine. It couldn't be true. It had to be a play for cash.

It was the only thing that made sense.

A loud cry tore from her little body and in a panic, I unfastened the harness around her and pulled her into my arms. "It's all right, little girl. I'll figure this out." I had no choice. This was exactly the kind of fuck up Jack had warned me about.

It took a few minutes to settle her down but when she stopped crying, I put her back in the carrier. She started crying again right away. We played this game for an hour before it became clear that she wouldn't go back to the carrier.

She was tiny and soft and smelled so sweet, which was probably how she got me to hold her all night.

Chapter 2

Sasha

Serenity stood with a smile when I entered her lavish office at Elite Nanny Service. "Sasha, I'm so glad you could make it in today. Have a seat and tell me, how are you doing?"

I couldn't help but smile at Serenity Majors. She was a beautiful woman with insane curves and an impeccable fashion sense. She looked like she belonged on the streets of New York City, not running a nanny agency in Houston. She was kind and nurturing, treating all of us as if we were members of her family. "Hey Serenity, you look fabulous as always."

"This old thing?" She laughed and brushed off my words with a smile and a blush. "So?"

"I'm good," I answered as I took the plush white chair in front of her desk. "I'm going to miss Jenna and James, but I'm so proud of them and happy for them." The twins

I'd been working with since they were one had officially started first grade and I was no longer needed. It was part of the job but that didn't make it hurt any less to say good-bye. "How are you?"

"Oh, you know. Busy as always but I love it." She flashed a beaming smile and laid her hand over a stack of files. "I have a few new families that might be a good fit for you. Interested or do you need a break?"

I took a moment to think about my answer. The truth was I hadn't been back to Connecticut to visit my family in more than a year, but that wasn't because I didn't have the time or the funds. It was because I didn't want to, not really. My family was complicated and that was putting it mildly so staying away was best for everyone, but most especially my mental health. "That depends on what you have for me," I answered.

Whatever Serenity was about to say was paused when the door behind me slammed open. I was on my feet in an instant, practically jumping over the glass desk to get behind my boss. My heart raced as I took in the giant blond man with broad shoulders and let out a shriek that brought all the attention to me.

"Who are you? What the hell are you doing, bursting in here like that?" My voice sounded shrill and anxious but that's exactly what I felt.

The large man had crazed green eyes and if not for the baby strapped to his body, he would've looked more terrifying simply due to his size. He was at least six feet, possibly six and a half feet, with broad shoulders, long, strong legs, and a power that emanated from him. That power was intimidating but it was also awesome. His gaze landed on Serenity. "You have to help me."

My heart still raced as Serenity stood and smoothed her hands over her red dress. "Have a seat, sir. I'm guessing you're new to parenthood?"

He nodded as his wild eyes darted around the room, the baby smiling and babbling against his chest. Finally, the big man sat and let out a long, expansive breath. "Less than twenty-four hours, in fact. The baby is good, perfect as long as I keep her in my arms, but the minute I put her down? She howls like a banshee."

Serenity laughed and put a hand to her chest as she settled a sweet gaze on the man and the little baby with a fiery crown of hair.

His blond brows dipped into a dark scowl. "It's no laughing matter. I need help and my friend says you are the best."

"I love to hear that. Who is your friend?"

"Dante Rush. You found him a nanny recently."

She nodded and walked around the desk, sitting on the edge with a grin. "If you know Dante then you know how I do things."

The man wasn't interested in the details, that was obvious by the set of his shoulders and the look of determination in green eyes that were exactly the same as the adorable baby girl fixed against his chest. "I didn't get the details from him but I can afford your fees and I'll pay it without negotiating. Please." Unlike so many of the entitled parents I've met and worked with over the years, this man had more of an air of desperation than entitlement. The baby started to cry in his arms but it started fussing and he pulled her closer, jostling her gently. "Please."

Serenity reached out and let one finger graze the soft tuft of red hair on the baby's head. "Sasha, you think you can take this sweetheart while I have a talk with Mr.?"

"Witter," he answered nervously, eyes darting back and forth. "Alex Witter."

I noticed that Serenity's gaze flashed at the name as if it was familiar to her but to me, he was just another handsome Texan, and my focus was on the baby girl in his arms.

I stared at the man a beat too long before her words registered. "Oh, sure." It was clear the man wasn't an actual threat so I relaxed and slowly made my way towards the blond giant, still wary but willing to help out. "Hey, sweet girl. I'm Sasha." I talked gently to the baby who turned her big green eyes to me, curious at first and then smiling excitedly. "That's right. I'm Sasha and we're going to hang out for a bit." I smiled at her and her smile grew as baby babble spilled from her rosebud lips.

When I reached for her, the man, Alex Witter, gripped her tight as if he was reluctant to let her go. "Careful. She tends to get a little fussy," he began when I scooped her from his arms and nestled her close. "I'll be damned. How did you do that?" His deep voice with a hint of a southern accent that was miles away from Texas was filled with awe.

I smiled at the man and really wished I hadn't because this close, he wasn't just handsome. He was breathtaking with green eyes, dotted with gold and dark gold specks. His skin held a hint of a tan like he spent a lot of time outdoors and his pink lips were full and his mouth, wide and kissable.

Wait, what? No, not kissable. Just noticeably plump.

"This is what I do, Mr. Witter." I glanced around in search of a diaper bag but when I found none, I held the baby closer and rushed from the office. Curiosity burned in my gut at the situation that brought the blond Viking to Elite Nanny Service. He was clearly out of place, not to mention out of his depths as a father, but why? Why was he so out of sorts? Was this the first time he'd been left alone with the child?

I took the baby to one of the meeting rooms stocked with everything a kid from aged one month to five years might need and changed her diaper. "You're a good little girl," I cooed while she kept up a steady stream of baby babble as I changed her, punching those chubby little legs as if she was going somewhere.

The big guy was a little on the gruff side but it was clear that whatever landed this little girl on his doorstep, he cared about her. It made me think of my own father, rich and short-tempered. He would have taken a belt to this little girl to get her to settle down. The idea of reaching out for professional help never would have occurred to him. "I guess in that way, you're lucky."

She laughed and continued kicking wildly.

"I hope you have a really great life, sweet girl. I really do." If her father was here, it meant he could afford to give her the best life had to offer, which made me smile. With the right start in life, a child could go far and though I barely knew her, that's what I hoped for this little girl.

Chapter 3

Alex

I stared across the desk at the well-dressed woman with a kind smile and thick sable hair, deciding whether or not to reveal all of my secrets to her. It was hard *not* to trust her when she looked at me as if she somehow understood everything I was going through. "Okay," I sighed and shook my head. "Someone dropped her on my doorstep last night with a note that said she was mine."

"Do you know who the mother is," she asked without judgment, which was what I really needed.

"No," I sighed and scrubbed a hand over my face. "She said she was dying and that she would be gone by the time I tracked her down, which takes a money grab off the table. *If* all of that is true, anyway." It was naïve, no, it was silly of me to reveal all of my secrets to a virtual stranger without asking her to sign a non-disclosure agreement. Jack was going to have my ass when he found out, and then he'd chew it up and spit it out when he heard everything.

Serenity sat back in her white leather seat and grinned. "I'm well aware of who you are, Mr. Witter and I can assure you that I have a reputation for being discreet."

My shoulders relaxed at her words. "That's good. But I have to warn you that my agent will probably come around in a few days with NDAs for you and the woman to sign."

She waved off my words with a laugh. "I can handle him, I assure you."

That was good because she would have to. "But, can you help me with my current predicament?" I looked over my shoulder at the door where the curvy raven-haired woman had exited from with my daughter. *Maybe* daughter my conscience corrected automatically. The DNA test was next on my list, just as soon as I could find some good help.

"I can."

"Good." I nodded and sat up a little taller, feeling more self-assured than I had since the little bundle of baby arrived on my doorstep. "I want her, the woman who has my daughter right now. She got her to stop crying."

She laughed. At me. No one ever laughed at Alex Witter. At least, not anymore. "You are lucky because Sasha has recently become available, but I'll have to check with her to see if she's willing to take on a job like this."

I frowned. "What does that mean? She's good with the

baby and she doesn't know who I am. I want her. It has to be her."

Serenity nodded. "Okay, assuming Sasha is available, what exactly are your needs?"

"I have no idea. I start training soon and I need someone who can be with her during the day while I'm training and to help me at night, at least until I get used to the responsibilities of fatherhood." A dark scowl crossed my face. "I sound like an asshole, right? If she's with the girl day and night, when will she sleep?"

She stood and placed a hand on my shoulder. It wasn't a come on or anything tawdry, it was just affectionate, possibly with a hint of pity. "There are live-in nannies, Mr. Witter."

"Alex. Call me Alex."

She nodded and took the chair right beside me. "A live-in nanny sounds like what you need, but I'll still need you to outline your needs so that Sasha can make an informed decision."

"Yeah, okay. This is all new to me. I don't know any babies, except my goddaughter and I'm more of an uncle. Not a father. I need help learning how to be a father as well as someone to take care of her while I'm away." At least until paternity was confirmed. After that? Hell, I had no idea.

"Sasha is one of my best, so if she decides to take this assignment she will be a valuable guide through parenthood for you."

I nodded because that was exactly what I needed. A guide. A daddy coach. "Perfect. I need her. Now."

"You're used to getting everything you want right when you want it, Mr. Witter."

"Yes." There was no point pretending otherwise.

"I understand but Sasha has a say in this as well."

Of course she did. "I'll double the pay."

Serenity's eyes widened in shock. "That may not be necessary. My nannies are paid very well."

"It is necessary," I insisted, feeling more confident as the words tumbled out of my mouth. "She doesn't know who I am yet, but you do. You know that in addition to the child, she will have to deal with tabloid journalists, paparazzi and wannabe groupies. She is definitely going to earn her salary, I promise that. Double the pay up front and if she wants or needs something else to do this, please tell me." I sounded like a desperate ass which was never a good negotiating position but I was desperate. I'd hardly gotten any sleep last night because I couldn't put the baby down without her bursting into tears. Sure, I dozed a few times in the recliner but anxiety made it difficult to get a good rest. I was desperate and willing to pay anything, hell to do just about anything to get that woman to be my nanny.

"So you're accepting paternity of the child?"

"For now, I am. I will have a rush done on paternity to make certain that she's mine but right now she needs to be cared for, so as right now, she's mine."

That seemed to please the woman because she

unleashed a smile that was full of pride and satisfaction. "I'll talk to Sasha and have an answer for you before the end of business today."

I wanted to tell her that wasn't good enough, that I didn't just need an answer *now* but I needed to take that woman, Sasha, home with me immediately. But there was a steely core to Serenity that was easy to see. She looked soft and feminine but she was no pushover and I'd end up worse than I was now if I pissed her off. "Okay, yeah. Thank you, Serenity."

"Don't worry, Alex. I will find you the perfect nanny. I promise."

I didn't have a lot of trust stored at the moment but when Serenity made that promise, I believed her. "Then I hope we'll be doing business together very soon."

She stood and walked with me to another room where the woman, Sasha was singing to my daughter who stared up at her as if she was the most interesting person she had ever seen. "Oh Alex, I have no doubt that we will."

Chapter 4

Sasha

I stood on the sidewalk before a tall glass and cement building that stretched into the clouds. It was the absolute height of luxury, I could tell as someone who grew up surrounded by it but even I was intimidated by the ostentatious display. It was a nice change of pace from the large mansions with acres of land that stretched in all directions that had dominated my professional life for the past decade, so I decided to embrace the difference.

It won't be so bad.

It couldn't possibly be all that bad since Mr. Witter was determined to pay me double what I'd made for the past five years. Serenity had assured me that I would earn the pay hike with all the extras that came with working for a man like Mr. Witter, but how could I turn down the opportunity to fatten my future savings? I couldn't. There would come a time, some day in the future—hopefully—

where my life would no longer accommodate a live-in nanny position, and I would have my savings to fall back on.

And your trust fund, that annoying bitch that lived in my subconscious reminded me the way she always did. Yes, I had a trust fund but in all the years since I left Connecticut, I'd only used it once. I lived on my salary and that was that. the fact that it pissed off my dad only made it feel *that much* better.

The day was sunny and warm but as I stepped into the black and silver marble lobby of Mr. Witter's building, I was instantly hit with a shot of cold air that sent a shiver down my spine. *It's not an omen,* I told myself and put on my best smile for the uniformed doorman with the salt and pepper hair. "Hi, Barry. I'm Sasha and I'm here for Mr. Witter."

He looked me up and down with a studious gaze that was almost offensive. "You're here for Mr. Witter?"

"I am. He's expecting me." I kept my smile in place because that's how I'd been trained my entire life but the disdain or maybe it was disbelief in his grey-green gaze put me on edge.

"I'm sorry, but I can't let you up." He didn't make a call or look at a list, which meant he was simply rejecting me.

"Mind telling me why?"

"Yes, I do mind, actually."

Oh, he wanted to play it that way? Okay. I was used to

people treating me a certain way because I was considered 'the help' or because I was a lot curvier than the average woman even down here in Texas, but that didn't mean I tolerated that nonsense. After all, I was Sasha Turner, daughter of the media mogul Bradley Rutherford Turner. No one treated me like that, not because I was someone important, but because I was someone, period. "What if I told you that Mr. Witter was expecting me?"

Barry tossed his head back and laughed. "You think you're the first woman to try that line with me, sweetheart? You're not which means you're not going up."

I frowned at his words. Did women often try to get inside Mr. Witter's apartment? I mean sure he was big and classically handsome with his shaggy blond hair and sparkling green eyes, but lying to get into his apartment was a bit much. Wasn't it?

"You should leave before you embarrass yourself, Miss."

That was it, that look of pity in his eyes pissed me off more than I could possibly explain. I leaned across the tall marble counter that kept him separate from the visitors, narrowed my gaze and lowered my voice. "Look, Barry, I don't know who you think I am or what you think my motives are and frankly I don't give a shit. But what I can tell you is that if I leave now, I'm not coming back and if that happens you will be the one out of a job. So please, for both of our sakes, call Mr. Witter and tell him that Sasha Turner is downstairs and she wishes entry to his apartment."

He sized me up for a long minute before deciding to hedge his bets and save his job, picking up the phone and talking discreetly into the receiver.

"Send her up," Alex barked loud enough that I heard him.

"Right away, sir." Barry turned to me with an apology in his eyes that I chose to ignore. "You have to understand," he began but I cut him off.

"I understand you have a job to do but I don't understand you treating me like less than a person based on your own personal opinion."

Without another word, he escorted me to the elevator, inserted a key, and pressed the large P that would take me to the penthouse. "It opens into the hallway and Mr. Witter's door is at the other end."

"Thank you." Just because he was a presumptuous pompous jerk didn't mean I had to be.

The elevator ride to the top lasted several minutes, at least that's what it felt like, or maybe it was just my nerves at starting a new job. Or, more likely, it was this particular job for the mysterious, handsome man who seemingly had a baby dropped into his lap. I decided on my way here that I wouldn't judge Alex. I didn't know his circumstances and as far as I could tell, he cared about my new charge. Nothing else was my business.

The doors slid open into a dimly lit hall that was black and silver just like the downstairs lobby. Step by step, I made my way towards the imposing black door, willing my heart to stop beating like this was a cause for worry. This was a job, an assignment like dozens of others I'd had over the years. There was no cause for alarm. Nothing to worry about.

I repeated those words over and over as I rapped on the door in five sharp knocks and waited.

The door flung open immediately and Mr. Witter appeared with wild, frantic eyes as he reached out and grabbed my wrist, yanking me inside. "Thank god you're here," he growled and then dropped my arm as if he just now realized his faux pas. "Sorry. But I'm glad you're here."

"It's all right. What's the problem?"

"Which one," he asked around a snort and scrubbed a hand down his face. It was then I noticed that Mr. Witter didn't have a shirt on. His chest and back were smooth and perfectly bronzed, like a statue. Covered in muscles and ink, he was a sight to behold as I followed him towards the sound of a baby crying. "This is the problem." He stepped aside and motioned towards the overstuffed sofa where the little girl laid on her back, naked with her feet kicking in the air.

I should have bitten back the laughter but it fell free before I could compose myself. Three discarded diapers dotted the sofa, each one more mangled than the previous.

"You've never changed a diaper."

"No." His answer was simple and plain, no excuses. I appreciated that.

"First, your sofa is far too nice to double as a changing table." But since it seemed that fatherhood was thrust upon him, I decided to cut him a break. "Do you have more diapers?"

"A few," he grumbled and handed me one. "They're tricky. Good luck."

I smiled at him and then down at the little girl who wore a sweet smile. "Okay, Mr. Witter, at first this seems impossible but after two or three diaper changes, you'll see it's nothing." To prove my point, I grabbed the baby at her ankles and slid the diaper underneath her, making use of the diaper ointment and baby powder on the coffee table beside me. "Front flap up, left sticker and then right sticker, and there you go!" I lifted the baby in the air, her legs and arms kicking as she cooed sweetly. "Fresh as a daisy."

"How did you do that?" His green eyes were wide with shock, a look of awe on his face.

"Like I said, it's easy once you know what you're doing. You'll catch on," I assured him as my gaze raked over his naked torso.

He seemed to realize just now that he was half naked. "She squirmed and nearly rolled off the sofa when I removed the dirty diaper and I didn't want her to fall."

I chuckled at his dismay. "That's why you need a changing table."

"I don't know what that is," he admitted easily, something I noticed that rich and powerful men had a hard time doing. "Make a list of what she needs. Please," he added belatedly.

I wanted to ask—badly—what in the hell had

happened that led to a clear bachelor taking care of a baby, but again, it wasn't my business. "I'll do that and maybe you can do something for me?"

He frowned as he raked one hand, and then the other, through his thick blond hair. "What's that?"

"Tell me her name. Babies respond better when they have a familiar word to answer to."

His brows furrowed. "I don't know. When she arrived, she didn't have one." His cheeks turned a bright shade of pink and he shook his head. "It's complicated but I guess I have to give her a name?"

I didn't want to add to his guilt or whatever else he was feeling, so I only nodded. "What did she come with?" It looked as if I would have to dive right into whatever this messy situation was, and it was lucky for Mr. Witter and his little girl that I handled messy like a pro.

"Just the bag," he said and pointed to a pale blue bag covered in daisies. "It had a few baby items in it but that was it."

"No note?"

"Attached to the carrier," he said absently.

The more pieces of the puzzle were revealed to me, the greater my sympathy for this situation became. "Do you mind," I asked and pointed to the bag.

He nodded.

I went through the bag to see if there was anything he'd forgotten because in my experience even the most detail oriented man tended to miss important things right in front of his face. I took inventory of what was left and it wasn't much, about five diapers, two bottles pre-filled with formula, a fresh pack of baby wipes, and a few onesies.

"Told you there was nothing."

I looked up at him with a smile as the little girl's head fell against my shoulder with a laugh. "Did you check all the pockets?" I didn't wait for an answer as I dug into the smaller zippered areas and found a pacifier with a plastic sunflower on it, a bottle of distilled water, several bottle cleaners and way in the bottom a sheet of paper. I slowly freed the sheet of paper and glanced down at what was a birth certificate but the mother's name was blacked out. "Her name is Dixie Summer Witter. She's about six months old, give or take a week."

He snatched the paper from my hands with an apologetic smile before he gave the document his full attention.

I watched in twisted fascination as at least a dozen different emotions splashed across his face. There was so much happening behind those green eyes and I was more curious than I should be about the details. Suddenly, every emotion melted away and left a blank stare in its place. He lifted his gaze to meet mine, something akin to embarrassment in his eyes. "I hate to do this so soon, but, ah, do you think you'll be all right on your own for a couple of hours? I need to talk to my agent immediately."

Agent. That was a big clue about what kind of big shot Mr. Witter was. "Sure." I frowned because I couldn't conjure up an image of him in anything I've seen recently. "You're an actor?"

Mr. Witter unleashed a beaming smile that made it

clear why he was a Hollywood heartthrob here in Texas. "No. I'm a hockey player."

Okay, now I was really confused. "There's hockey in Houston?"

Mr. Witter's smile faded and I worried, for a moment, that I might have offended him. But a beat later, a loud laugh exploded out of him, startling both me and Dixie. "I promise to be offended by that later but for now, I really need to head out."

"Dixie and I will be fine for a couple of hours but this isn't enough to even get us through the night." I patted the daisy diaper bag on the sofa to remind him that this wasn't something we could postpone.

"Yeah, okay," he nodded absently, clearly distracted. "This first and then baby supplies." He slipped into a pair of sneakers and grabbed his eyes.

"Uh, Mr. Witter?"

He stopped and studied me. "Call me, Alex. You'll be living in my home, no need to be so formal."

"Okay then, Alex. You might want to put on a shirt before you head out."

He looked down at his sculpted bare chest and grinned. "Good idea. Thank you, Sasha. You're already helping." He disappeared down the hall and returned a few minutes later in a fresh pair of jeans and a black t-shirt, looking like a big, beautiful, blond Viking before he rushed out of the apartment.

I turned to Dixie who was still studying my face with a

ghost of a smile on her lips. "It's just you and me for a while, kiddo. Let's get to know each other." I held her close and get acquainted with my new work and living space.

* * *

Check out the rest of Sasha & Alex's story!

Also by Piper Sullivan

Nanny Series

Curvy Fake Wife for the Player

Curvy Nanny for the Grumpy Single Dad

Small Town Lovers

Midlife Baby: Morgot & Grady

Midlife Fake Out: Bella & Derek

Midlife Love Affair: Lacy & Levi

Midlife Valentine: Valona & Trey

Midlife Do Over: Pippa & Ryan

Healing Love

Dueling Drs, Book 6: Zola & Drew

Rockstar Baby Daddy, Book 5: Susie & Gavin

Unfriending the Dr, Book 4: Persy & Ryan

Kissing the Dr, Book 3: Megan & Casey

Loving the Nurse, Book 2: Gus & Antonio

Falling for the Dr, Book 1: Teddy & Cal

Curvy Girl Dating Agency

Forever Curves, Book 8: Brenna & Grant

Small Town Curves, Book 7: Shannon & Miles

Curvy Valentine Match, Book 6: Mara & Xander

Misbehaving Curves, Book 5: Joss & Ben

Curves for the Single Dad, Book 4: Tara & Chris

His Curvy Best Friend, Book 3: Sophie & Stone

Curvy Girl's Secret, Book 2: Olive & Liam

His Curvy Enemy, Book 1: Eva & Oliver

Small Town Protectors (Tulip Series)

That Hot Night, Book 12: Janey & Rafe

To Catch A Player, Book 11: Reece & Jackson

Cold Hearted Love, Book 10: Ginger & Tyson

Hero Boss, Book 9: Stevie & Scott

Dr's Orders, Book 8: Maxine & Derek

Mastering Her Curves, Book 7: Mikki & Nate

Kissing My Best Friend, Book 6: Bo & Jase

Undesired, Book 5: Hope & Will

Wanting Ms Wrong, Book 4: Audrey & Walker

Loving My Enemy, Book 3: Elka & Antonio

Bad Boy Benefits, Book 2: Penny & Ry

Hero In My Bed, Book 1: Nina & Preston

Accidental Hookups

Accidentally Hitched, Book 1: Viviana & Nash

Accidentally Wed, Book 2: Maddie & Zeke

Accidentally Bound, Book 3: Trish & Mason

Accidentally Wifed, Book 4: Magenta & Davis

Boardroom Games

His Takeover: An Enemies to Lovers Romance (Boardroom Games Book 1)

Sinful Takeover: An Enemies to Lovers Romance (Boardroom Games Book 2)

Naughty Takeover: An Enemies to Lovers Romance (Boardroom Games 3)

Boxsets & Collections

Small Town Misters: A Small Town Protectors Boxset

Misters of Pleasure: A Small Town Protectors Boxset

Misters of Love: A Small Town Romance Boxset

Misters of Passion: A Small Town Romance Boxset

Kiss Me, Love Me: An Alpha Male Romance Boxset

Accidentally On Purpose: A Marriage Mistake Boxset

Daddies & Nannies: A Contemporary Romance Boxset

Cowboys & Bosses: A Contemporary Romance Boxset

About the Author

Piper Sullivan is an old school romantic who enjoys reading romantic stories as much as she enjoys writing them.

She spends her time day-dreaming of dashing heroes and the feisty women they love.

Visit Piper's website www.pipersullivan.com

Join Piper's Newsletter for quirky commentary, new romance releases, freebies and contests.

Check her out on BookBub

Stalk her on Facebook

Made in United States
Troutdale, OR
09/16/2024

22886887R00159